A Wonderful Piece of Work

Stephen Curtis

Published by Kingsway Publishing, Bath 2014

Kingsway Publishing, Bath
3 Kingsway,
Bath, BA2 2NH
UK

email: KingswayPubBath@aol.com

ISBN: Paperback 978-0-9931312-0-2

eBook-Kindle 978-0-9931312-1-9

Second impression

Antony: Would I had never seen her!

Enobarbus: O, sir, you had then left unseen a wonderful piece of work ...

Antony and Cleopatra Act I scene 2

Part 1

Making

1

'It is you, isn't it?'

It was 1984. I was in Liberty's during my lunch hour, looking for a birthday present for my mother in ladies' accessories or whatever they call the department where they sell scarves. I was fingering some silky stuff in a familiar rich print when an expensively dressed woman wearing a headscarf in a similar print and a very large pair of dark glasses planted herself beside me and directed this question at me out of the corner of her mouth.

'I don't know' I replied in a normal voice. 'Who are you?'

She raised her sunglasses briefly, then lowered her head. 'It's me. Beatrice.'

'Beatrice Williams, my God!'

'Keep your voice down! Tell me your name, and I'll remember you exactly.'

'Nigel Anderson.' I said, automatically adopting the same furtive tone. 'How are you? What's going on?'

'I'm escaping from my husband. I need a friend. You shouldn't have grown a beard, Nigel Anderson, it confuses people. I had to watch you for ages before I was sure it was you.'

'But what …?'

'I'm escaping from my husband. Do you think I usually go around looking like the Queen in a Land Rover? Don't look up! Are there any large Americans in here?'

'How can I see without looking up? I don't think so.'

'Can I help you, sir, madam?' A shop assistant approached us.

'No, thank you. We're just looking.' I said.

'If madam's not interested in buying the scarf and the sunglasses, perhaps I could put them back for her?'

I hadn't noticed that those items still had the price tags on.

'My friend's buying them for me.'

'Then if you wouldn't mind coming this way.' I think that from anyone else there might have been a glance of mute appeal at this stage, some gesture that said 'I'm in a jam, please help'. But Bea, still keeping her head down, simply followed the assistant, and I simply followed her.

This sort of thing didn't usually happen in the lunch hour; she was, presumably, in distress; and I did know her … well, I knew her of old, so to speak. It was at least eight years since I'd last seen her at university, but she had imprinted herself very firmly on my memory there. Who didn't remember Bea Williams?

'Forty-five pounds seventy pence, please, sir. Cash or card?'

They were designer sunglasses, and the scarf was silk.

'(Gulp!) Card.'

Bea hustled me towards the Regent Street end of the store.

'I saw him as I was coming up Regent Street. I don't know whether he saw me … Oh God, there he is.'

'Which one is he?'

'The tall one talking to the man in the black hat. Don't look at him.'

'Beatrice, he doesn't know me from a bar of soap.'

'Well, he knows me, and he bought me this outfit. What's he doing?'

'I think he's going to cross the road.'

'Oh, Christ!'

She grabbed me by the hand and towed me upstairs, over the bridge, through various departments, down some more stairs, and out at the other end of the store. We had scuttled half way down Carnaby Street and were well mingled in with the crowd, before Bea, after several glances over her shoulder, decided it was safe to slow down.

'Would you take me somewhere? I'm starving and dying for a coffee.'

I knew the area well, having worked nearby for a number of years. I steered her down a side street to a quiet café. She selected a table where she would not be seen from the window and sat down.

'Well, it's nice to see you again ... but would you mind explaining what the hell is going on?'

'In a minute. Comfort food, please.' This was to the waitress. 'Steak, medium rare, sausages, chips, fried egg, onions, anything else that goes with it, and a large coffee, and make it as quick as you can, I'm in a hurry.'

The waitress looked at me.

'A cream cheese and tomato sandwich and a coffee, please.'

'As quick as you can, please.'

The waitress disappeared into the kitchen.

'I have to be back at work in ...' I looked at my watch, 'about twenty minutes.'

'I am in such trouble,' she said, still in a low voice as if one of the other customers or one of the staff might betray her. 'The bastard's stopped all my credit cards. I don't have any money.'

'Can't you go to your parents?'

'He'll be watching their house. Anyway, they don't know I'm in England — unless he's been there already. Ugh, ghastly man!'

'You make him sound like the godfather or something.'

'Yes, that's it. Exactly. Have you got a cigarette?'

'Sorry, I've given up.'

'Bugger! This is the only pack I've got.' She took a packet out of her bag and lit up.

'Let me get this straight. You're married to an American Mafia boss; you're running away from him; he's chasing you around London; and you haven't got any money.'

'Yes.'

'Where are you staying?'

'The Dorchester. That's where we always stay in London. That was my big mistake. He must have gone straight there. I can't go back, it's out of the question.'

'But what can he do to you?'

'Use your imagination! ... Thank you, can I have some tomato ketchup?'

She tucked into her steak and chips as if she really hadn't eaten for a week. It was such an unlikely story. And yet, Bea was one of those people with whom the unlikely becomes all too likely. She hadn't changed much in herself — as far as I could see behind the sunglasses and the scarf, which she had not removed. Her teeth were the same — 'borrowed from a horse', as my friend RT used to say. But the casual, slightly eccentric gear she favoured at university had been replaced by what looked to me like the quintessence of chic. It had evidently set someone back, presumably her allegedly gangster husband, a great many dollars.

'What are you going to do?' I asked when she had finished.

'I don't know. I have to find somewhere to stay to give me a chance to think things over.' She looked at me.

'No, I'm sorry. I can't put you up.'

'I wasn't thinking of asking *you*.'

'Also, I have to be back at work in five minutes. Do you want anything else?'

'Are you married?'

'No.'

'Are you living with someone?'

'No.'

'I knew I'd see *someone* in London. Everyone's here now, aren't they?'

'Depends who you mean by everyone. None of the people I knew at university are here. Well, there's one chap I knew slightly ... Could I have the bill, please?'

'Where are you working?'

'At a publisher's in Golden Square. It's five minutes from here. Look, I have to go, I've got a meeting at half past two.'

'You can't be very senior if you're so fussy about timekeeping.'

'I hoped I'd make managing director by thirty, but I didn't. Now, are you going to be all right?'

'It should be bloody obvious I'm not going to be all right.'

'Then what do you expect me to do?'

'I don't know. I don't know what to do. Oh God!' And she began to cry.

The waitress brought the bill. I paid. Bea was still crying. The waitress presumably thought it was some kind of couple crisis. 'Can I bring you something else?' she asked. 'A glass of water?'

'No', I said, 'thanks. She's upset.' The waitress retreated and watched us from behind the counter.

'Oh God!' said Beatrice again and drummed her fists on the table.

'Look,' I said, 'calm down. I really do have to go. Take this.' I handed her a ten-pound note, one of the two I had in my wallet. 'If you're desperate ...'

'I *am* desperate. Can't you see I'm desperate?'

'If you're desperate, meet me after work and we'll try and work out what to do.'

'Where's that?'

'Walk down with me now, and I'll show you.'

I dare say that little scene must have intrigued the waitress and the couple of other diners. I hurried Bea off down an alleyway and some side streets. She clacked along beside me in high heels, holding onto my arm and keeping her face averted. When we reached Golden Square, I showed her the building where my firm's offices were.

'I'll be out as soon as I can after five o'clock. I'll wait in the square until half past five or quarter to six. If you're not there by then, I'll assume you've got something else sorted out.'

'How can I contact you?'

I fumbled for a business card, and scribbled my home number on the other side.

'OK? Look, I'm sorry, I have to go.'

'What shall I do?'

'Find somewhere quiet and try and think things out. Now, I'm late already. I may see you later.'

I thought about fishing out my wallet again and giving her the other tenner — then thought again. I went inside and dashed off up the stairs leaving her standing rather forlornly on the pavement.

2

I found it even more difficult than normal to concentrate on the matters being discussed at the meeting. I wasn't sure whether I hoped that Bea would disappear as suddenly as she had arrived, or that she would be there again at five o'clock. And this despite the fact that it looked very much as though she meant trouble, and, in fact, bigger and more serious trouble, quite possibly, than she used to cause when I knew her earlier.

It was a pretty slack time in my life, hence the fact that a little excitement was not unwelcome. To be honest, it was worse than slack. It seemed that nothing significant was happening to me and that I really wasn't going anywhere.

When I left university, I didn't have to wait too long before being offered a job with the publishing company in Golden Square. I wasn't entirely sure it was what I wanted, but it seemed like too good an opportunity for an English graduate to pass up. All the people I knew in the literary line said they were green with envy. Moreover, it fitted in well with my love life. Hilary, my girlfriend from university days, had decided that she would follow in her parents' footsteps and teach. She would live at home for a year and take her diploma in London.

For that year Hilary and I saw a great deal of one another and had, I thought, a wonderful time. By the end of it I had found a nice flat, big enough for both of us, but she, of course, needed a job. She was offered one in Chester and took it. I was disappointed, but it was a good school, and she said a year spent in the vicinity of her mother had convinced her that London was not the place for her. So we were reduced to seeing each other only during holidays and at weekends. I bought myself a little Citroen 2CV to commute in. Still, we knew we were serious about one another. We said we were serious about one another. Everyone acknowledged that it was a really serious affair and expected us to get married or at least set up house together on a permanent basis.

Geography began to tell in the second year of our separation. It was difficult saving all one's significant social and emotional life for weekends. In summer 1979 we went on holiday to southern France. I was hoping we'd light upon somewhere quiet and romantic. But the hilltop village with the small characterful hotel and the best undiscovered restaurant in Europe failed to materialize. The Citroen boiled. The tent — carried solely for emergencies — blew down in a thunderstorm. And whereas before we might have made light of all this, treating the mishaps as things to laugh about and dine out on later, now we got fed up — fed up with the heat, the horse-flies, the discomfort, and, in the end, with each other. Even that needn't have been fatal, if Hilary and I had simply said to ourselves: 'this is about having a bad holiday, these things happen'. But we didn't. We took it as a symptom of a malaise affecting our relationship — but not the same malaise.

I thought things were going badly because we'd delayed making a proper commitment to one another — so I proposed. She was convinced things were going badly because our relationship had run its course — so she turned me down. And she told me there was someone else waiting in the wings, and a year or so later she married him.

And that was that — except that my whole life seemed suddenly to have been turned upside down and emptied out.

By the time of my re-encounter with Bea, more than four years on from this break-up, I was officially over it. I was settled in London and my job. I had a few new friends. I had moved on — not very far, but on. The only relic of my deep and very painful disappointment over Hilary was a kind of septic 'what-forism'. If any major question came up I would think it over, debate it with myself, get mildly excited, but when the first excitement ebbed I would ask — what for? In those days, there was never a convincing answer;

consequently, the usual result was inaction. I stayed in the same job, or at least with the same company; I stayed in the same flat; I kept to the same smallish circle of acquaintances; I didn't attempt to get serious with women.

Bea Williams most definitely did not fall into the category of women I might get serious with — not by any stretch of the imagination.

I had met her, as I have said, at university. The new university that we both attended had then been in existence for less than ten years. It was architecturally undistinguished — consisting, essentially, of four squat blocks in a field with car parks and a main building modelled on a famous Swedish crematorium. Its principal feature was a lake populated by ducks of various descriptions — an elegant solution to the drainage problem on the site made available by the city fathers. The teaching staff were not dull. They were mostly young, knew their stuff, and taught well. In dress and behaviour they followed the style of the times; they were casual, relaxed, approachable, and affable. But there were no eccentrics. There was no-one who took potshots at the ducks from upstairs windows; no-one who had wild hair and staring eyes, who dressed like a bag lady, who took lectures with their flies open or using a megaphone; there were not even many drunks. There was a distinct lack of material for a lifetime of anecdotes. That was where Bea came in.

She complemented her distinctive looks with distinctive dress and with a style of speech and behaviour that ranged from the highly sophisticated to the outrageous. She was at various times reputed to be having affairs with everyone from the vice-chancellor to the Spanish language assistant — a Mexican with an enormous Afro. She was said to have refused an invitation from the Photographic Society to pose as Ophelia in a reedy section of the lake, but it was generally known that she was happy to pose nude for them indoors. She took eighteen months off from her course to go to

California and try to make it in movies and nobody among the teaching or administrative staff batted an eyelid. Bea appeared to live in rather lurid technicolour, while the rest of us existed in monochrome.

She did return to university from the US, but gave the distinct impression that she had been dragged back to the north of England much against her will. It was written all over her: 'I have swum with dolphins, sharks, great whales, and the myriad brilliant creatures of the coral reefs — what am I doing now back in this shabby lake with the minnows and a few old trout?' But, as part of her attempt to get through the boredom, she took up with one of the best friends I have ever had and — quite incidentally, I'm sure, on her part — killed the friendship stone dead.

Arthur Llewellyn James was my friend's name, except he hated the name Arthur and insisted on being referred to as RT (as in Artie!). The university brought us together by chance as roommates in one of the residential blocks on campus, but we hit it off from the beginning and for the best part of three years did most things together.

RT was Welsh. As a biology student he owned a pair of binoculars for observing wildlife through the window of the room we shared, which was on the top floor. He had the bed closest to the window, and would often collect all the pillows and cushions in the room and make them into a kind of ramp up to the bedhead. He would then lie on his stomach propped up on this ramp looking out of the window through his binoculars for hours at a time. He was genuinely interested in birds and liked watching the ducks. At the same time he was a normal, red-blooded, heterosexual student and, if there was nothing doing in duckland, he was quite happy watching the woman traffic along the lakeside. 'Got a gorgeous bird in view,' he announced one day. 'Long blonde hair, blue eyes, big boots, I can't do a proper tits assessment because she's wearing a big woolly jacket. Big teeth she has, stolen from a horse by the look of it. And she's actually having a set-to with this half-naked bloke.'

That was almost my first sight of Bea. I had noticed her before in the vicinity of English classes. She was about to break up in spectacular fashion with her current lover, a tall, bony, bearded man dressed that day only in a pair of tattered jeans and a tee shirt. In full view of us (and many other people, no doubt) Bea expostulated with him, swore at him, then begin hitting him, harder and harder, until eventually he lost his temper. He slapped her across the face with a force that shook her rigid. Her glasses fell off. She put her hand to her cheek and stared, while he looked momentarily stunned by his own action.

At that point, we leapt up and pelted down the stairs. We could not simply watch this, we had to help. We might be the only witnesses; he might hit her again.

But we were not the only witnesses. There was quite a large group of students, teachers and general staff surrounding Bea and the man. We saw him led off in one direction and her in another. She was taken to hospital for a precautionary check (her face was a mess and she thought he might have dislodged one of her teeth).

Somehow RT managed to get himself into the party taking Bea away on a stretcher. She was sitting inside the ambulance with blood on her face, pale and shocked out of her ordinary self-confidence. Their eyes met. Bea, as I may have said, has extraordinarily striking blue eyes. He imprinted on her ... or, as he himself put it, he felt the finger the fate.

The finger of fate lay fairly lightly on him while Bea, partly as a result of that incident, was away in California. Before I got together with Hilary, RT was already going out with her friend Caroline, a lanky girl with a face that looked slightly lopsided from a habit she had of carrying her head at a slight angle. She was taller than RT — he was quite stocky and slightly less than medium height — and with her hair scraped back in a pony tail, wearing little make-up, with a flat chest and big hands and feet, she was not good-looking. But the essential Caroline, I felt, was anything but unattractive. She had very dark brown eyes and an intense way of looking at you. In addition, she was a very lively talker, ironic, funny, and extremely intelligent. Most of all, she absolutely adored RT; it just shone out of her. She was transfigured when she was around him.

And then Bea came back. I was having lunch with Caroline and Hilary in a dining room that also overlooked the lake on the day when RT fulfilled his fate and got off with her — in full view of the three of us. Their affair didn't last long, didn't end in violence — they had a noisy row outside an English seminar room that ended with Bea screaming with laughter when she found out that RT's real name was Arthur — and it didn't even kill off RT's relationship with Caroline (they got married a couple of years after finishing university), but it made me very angry. I remonstrated with him about his treatment of Caroline; he told me in no uncertain terms how boring and moralistic I was and what a drag I had been on him all through our time at university. Punches were thrown. We barely spoke afterwards. He deliberately avoided saying goodbye after the graduation ceremony.

I didn't exactly blame Bea for that, but it didn't endear her to me. However 'exciting' and 'colourful' life around her might be, I didn't want to be drawn in. But, I reassured myself, it was all right. If I needed a way out, I had one.

It was 1984, the year of the miners' strike. My younger brother, Dave, had been radicalized by Voluntary Service Overseas and doing a politics degree. When he left university he worked for an outfit called Rural Revival III (RRIII for short), something between a charitable organization and a political pressure group. By the time of Bea's reappearance, Dave was inhabiting a tiny cottage in deepest Linconshire with two large dogs, a goat, several cats, a stray parrot, and his heavily pregnant wife of six months, Maisie.

Strictly speaking, RRIII, a purist ecological group, was against the consumption of fossil fuels. It looked forward to the withering away of the coalmining industry — and most other industry — in a wind- and wave-powered future. But in the present situation, given the total indifference of Mrs Thatcher to everything that RR III stood for and given their sense that, not content to let the coalmining industry wither away, she was set on extirpating it and its attendant village communities root and branch, RRIII solemnly declared its solidarity with the National Union of Mineworkers.

Dave was not averse to mixing a bit of carnivorous action into his generally herbivorous lifestyle. He frequently cycled over to pits in north Notts or south Yorks and joined the picket line. Once the men in boots and donkey jackets got used to the presence of a lettuce-eater on a bike who looked a lot like Jesus, and discovered that he was quite prepared to mix it with the police, they took to him. Furthermore, when they found out that he knew a bit about practical politics, they even admitted him to some of their tactical discussions. And when the proposal came up to widen the struggle and send miners around the country to spread the word and collect funds — in particular, to send miners to London to protest outside Parliament, the TUC headquarters, etc, Dave spoke up and said 'I have a brother with a flat in London. He can put a couple of comrades up'.

So, while mulling over my encounter with Bea instead of concentrating on whether it would be a good idea to produce a series of books on 'Great Business Minds of the Twentieth Century', and while trying to decide whether or not I wanted her to be in Golden Square when I finished work at five o'clock, I was confident of one thing at least. If she did try to wangle her way into my flat for the night, I had a cast-iron excuse to put her off. 'I've got two striking miners staying in the spare bedroom!'

3

She came. Not at five o'clock, but only just outside the time frame I'd set for waiting for her in the square.

'Are you all right?'

'No, I'm worn out.'

'What have you been doing?'

'Feeding the pigeons in the fucking park! What do you expect me to do with ten quid?'

'Have you seen him again — your husband?'

'Rich? No. Bastard! This is terrible, I've no money, I've had nothing to eat, I've nowhere to stay …'

'Have you had any thoughts?'

'No.'

'Then what are you going to do?'

'I don't know what I'm going to do.'

'Well, you can't stay out here all night.'

'Where did you say you live?'

'No, I'm sorry. I've got two spare miners staying in my bedroom.'

'What?' she said, then she burst out laughing. 'God!' she said, 'I haven't laughed in weeks. Two spare miners?'

'I meant …' and I explained as briefly as I could what I did mean, and endeavoured to fuse the ice that had been broken back together again.

'But I don't mind. I like Yorkshire people' Bea protested. 'I was there the same as you. I haven't heard anyone say "eeh by gum!" in ages.'

'Bea, nobody actually says "eeh by gum!"'

'Don't be pedantic. Anyway, it'll give me a chance to see where you live.'

'Why should you be the least bit interested in seeing where I live? Forgive me for being blunt, but have you actually given me any thought at all between the last time we saw each other at university and today in Liberty's? Have you?'

'I don't forget my former lovers and I hope they don't forget me.' She stopped dead on the pavement, causing the crowd to part and pass on either side of us, and quoted solemnly, though with a slightly different emphasis than the poet intended. '*I* am a part of all that I have met ...'

To which I replied, continuing the quotation: 'Yet all experience is an arch wherethrough ...' and she joined in to carry it through to the end of the sentence: 'Gleams that untravelled world, whose margin fades / For ever and for ever when I move.'

Two English graduates communing through Tennyson's *Ulysses* amid the rush-hour crowd close to one of the entrances to Piccadilly Circus station with it just coming on to rain — a bad Hollywood moment.

'Thank you for sharing that with me, Bea. There's just one thing. I am not one of your former lovers.'

'Yes you are.'

'I'm not.'

'You are. I ought to know.'

'You ought to know, but you obviously don't.'

'You are. We had a tremendous row outside a seminar room ... that drippy lecturer Bill Bailey or something was there.'

'That wasn't me, it was my friend RT, RT James, Arthur ... don't you remember him?'

'Arthur ... oh yes, yes, him!' And she threw her head back and shrieked with laughter all over again, till she suddenly stopped. 'Mustn't call attention to myself,' she said, belatedly remembering the supposed drama of the situation. 'Can we go into the station? I'll be less visible and I'm getting wet.'

I didn't really want to go into the station because it was another step closer to taking Bea home with me, but it was now raining quite hard and everybody else was pushing to get down the stairs and under cover, so I had to go with the flow.

'If you weren't my lover,' said Bea as we emerged into the big circular concourse, 'how come I know you so well?'

'You don't know me very well.'

'Yes I do. I feel I do. We must have been soulmates then. There must have been a primal sympathy, "which having been must ever be". Wait a bit. I've got some change from the ten pounds you gave me, I'll buy myself a ticket from the machine. Where to?'

'Bea, stop. We have to sort this out. You can't stay in my flat, there isn't any room.'

'I know, the spare miners. I don't mind sleeping with you. My marriage is over.'

'That's not the point. What about your things?'

'They're at the Dorchester. I can't go back there. Rich will be there and, even if he isn't, I can't pay the bill. It doesn't matter, I sleep in the nude. I'll clean my teeth with my finger.' She stuck her finger in her mouth and looked at me coquettishly.

'It's not my problem. The long and the short of it is, Bea, that it's not my problem.'

There was a pause. Then, characteristically, she changed her line of attack.

'I see. You're enjoying this, aren't you?'

'I'm just telling you the truth. It isn't my problem.'

'The truth is you're abandoning me to my fate in the middle of London with people after me and not a penny to my name.'

'Why should I feel guilty about a situation you got yourself into — especially since you only bumped into me by chance.' Surely that was unanswerable.

'Men are such bastards ... usually such bastards. I really didn't think you were like that.'

'You don't know me.'

'Fine. Fine … I've got your card. I'll send you the ten pounds when I've got it …'

'Don't worry about the money.'

'No. I'm sure I can go on the streets or something. Goodbye, Nigel, it was nice meeting you again.' She held out her hand to me; we shook hands. She turned and started to walk away.

Of course, she did know me … or she knew her men.

'Bea …!'

4

The two spare miners were called Steve and Brian. They were father and son. Brian, who was about twenty-three, had followed his father into the pit. I'm not sure that he had ever been to London before — at least not since he was grown up. The sights of London were a considerable distraction for him from the task in hand. He was full of wide-eyed curiosity and fascinated by everything that was going on. His father, in his late forties, was a bit dour and sombre. I think he had a sense that he was fighting a losing battle this time. He also knew that if the pit closed and he lost his job, it would be extremely difficult to get another one at his age.

When Bea and I arrived back at the flat, Brian was sitting on the sofa in the living room, waiting for his turn to use the bathroom. They wore their usual working clothes from the mine when they went out and had been told to black their hands, faces, and clothes up a bit to ensure that the public recognized them as miners and had the impression that they had come straight from the coalface to the capital. Brian had carefully spread a sheet of newspaper under himself before he sat down. He stood up when he saw Bea.

'Hello, Brian. This is a friend of mine — er, from university — Beatrice, Bea. Do you prefer people to call you Beatrice or Bea?'

'Bea, whatever … Hi, Brian!'

Safely inside the flat, Bea at last removed her headscarf and dark glasses and shook out her long blonde hair. She was still a stunner. Brian was suitably stunned.

'Hello … I won't …' He stretched out his grimy hand towards her and jerked it back again. Steve emerged from the bathroom in his vest and pants, spotted Bea, and immediately withdrew again. 'Brian …!' he called.

'I'll just get …' said Brian, realizing his father wanted some clothes and realizing at the same time that it wasn't a good idea to pick them up with dirty hands.

'What does he want?' I asked.

'There's a shirt and trousers out on the bed. Could you give them to him?'

I went to help Steve, while Brian continued to stare at Bea.

'Do you want to sit down?' he asked, moving the newspaper to one end of the sofa and gesturing towards the other. Then, deciding that perhaps he'd better not share space with Bea at all until he had cleaned himself up, he stood and hovered awkwardly near the bathroom door.

'Don't let me get in anyone's way,' said Bea.

Steve emerged, decently dressed. I introduced him to Bea. Brian darted into the bathroom. When he came out, I offered them all a drink and tried to think of what to give them to eat.

'If you were wanting a private party like,' said Steve, 'we'll get out of your way. We can pop down the road for a burger or something.'

'No, it's OK. Bea's staying the night — just tonight. It's — er — it's a sort of an emergency. She's had a bit of trouble.'

'Oh, right.'

I exited to the kitchen, leaving them to talk, half-listening through the open door. In my years in London I had become reasonably competent domestically. In the early days, my mother had insisted on coming up to town to 'do for me' at regular intervals. To dissuade her, I had had to get her to teach me a few of the skills she would never have thought of passing on at home. I was able to knock up a reasonably edible risotto and such like at short notice.

Steve and Brian were telling Bea how they spent their day and what sort of reaction they got from Londoners when they were leafleting or collecting.

'Ordinary folk are OK. They sympathize, and they'll usually give you something too. But the bloody yuppies … we've had some abuse, I can tell you.'

'Posh women are the worst …' said Brian, then stopped and blushed.

'Don't worry about me,' said Bea. 'I'm only posh on the outside. These are posh,' indicating her clothes, 'I haven't got a penny.'

They looked at her sceptically.

'Really, I haven't. But go on with what you were saying.'

'They slag you off. This one, she could have been a model — only young, very smart, big hat, little dog, she comes right up to my dad and she says "you effing wrecker, you're effing ruining this country, you effing this, you effing that, I hope you effing starve." Right in his face. You don't expect that from the upper classes.'

'It's not the language,' said Steve, 'it's the hatred. But I suppose back home everyone hates the scabs and the police.'

'The police are right bastards. They goad you. They want you to throw stones, so they've got an excuse to come and bash your head in. My pal had to have ten stitches.'

'But you're all right?'

'Not a mark on me — anywhere. I got a pickaxe handle that's as good as any bloody police baton.'

'Any road' said Steve, changing the subject, perhaps on the mistaken assumption that Bea would know nothing at all about physical violence, 'what do you think about all this?'

'All this?'

'The strike.'

'Well, I've been in America. I don't know much about it.'

'Aren't they following it over there?' asked Brian. 'It's bloody big news over here, I can tell you.'

'They hardly know England exists. Outside the big cities, people used to ask me if I was Australian, so I got fed up with that and I tried to sound as American as possible — meet me at de coyner of toidy toid 'n toid.'

'If they thought you were Australian, it's because you're blonde and bloody gorgeous, love. Anyway, what's America like? Is it like it is in the films?'

Bea tucked her legs under her on the sofa and prepared to be the centre of attention.

* * *

She was still the centre of attention after the meal, when we were well into a second bottle of wine. I could see that Brian was in two minds whether to ask to switch on the TV to get the latest news, but listening to her was much more interesting. And she was just getting on to the subject of her differences with her husband.

'... His family's immensely wealthy, of course, and so is he.'

'Rich by name and rich by nature.'

'Exactly, Brian. He has a house on Long Island, an apartment in New York City, a beach house on the Atlantic and another one on the Pacific. There's a Guildersleeve Center, a Guildersleeve university somewhere, and this big thing called the Guildersleeve Trust, which controls it all. It's an incredible organization.'

'And you gave all that up?'

'I didn't own any of it. None of it was mine. All I had was him, and he's completely dysfunctional.'

'Oh ... dis- what?'

'He's a bloody nutcase,' explained Steve.

'He's cold, he's mean, he has to be in control of everything, and all he thinks about is making money. I was going completely mad.'

'Why did you marry him in the first place?' I asked.

'It was my biggest mistake ever, ever! And, as you probably remember, I've not been exactly … I've had a bit of a chequered career.'

'All right then, if it's not a rude question, why did he marry you?'

'I should have thought that was bloody obvious,' chipped in the gallant Brian.

'He wanted children. It's pointless having all that wealth if you don't carry on the line, and his younger brother had already started a brood, which would eventually have put him higher in the pecking order if Rich couldn't succeed in reproducing himself. His first wife couldn't have any, so he was in the process of ditching her when he met me. He likes blondes, he thinks English people are classy … we do have a certain *cachet* on the East Coast, where they know the difference between the English and the Australians — and he had me checked out by a bunch of doctors and, I'm happy to tell you, gentlemen, that all my egg-laying equipment is in perfect working order. Also, I suppose, because I was a foreigner and not fabulously wealthy, he thought I'd be more biddable. Does that answer your question, Nigel?'

'And now you've run away from him?' said Steve.

'Yes.'

'And he's come after you?'

'He's here in London, yes.'

'Well, doesn't that show he wants you back?'

'Did you actually have any children?' I put in before she could answer.

'No. And I'm not sure it's me that he wants back.'

'What do you mean?'

'I don't know if I should tell you this … I brought some things with me from the New York apartment when I left.'

'What sort of things?'

'He's an art collector …'

'Oh my God, Bea …!'

'I needed some insurance.'

'Are they valuable?'

'Priceless, I hope.' She lit a cigarette.

'Well, if you left them at the hotel, he'll have found them by now.'

'I didn't. They aren't at the hotel.'

'Bloody hell!' said Brian and whistled.

'Where are they?' I asked.

'They're safe.'

'Isn't that stealing?' Steve put the obvious question.

'I'm not going to keep them. I said I wanted insurance,' Bea replied sedately. 'Before we got married, I had to sign a marriage contract, which basically said I wouldn't get any money if we got divorced. I had to put up with him trying to impregnate me for three years; I reckon I deserve something.'

'Yes,' said Steve. 'Well, it's all a bit different from "for richer, for poorer, for better, for worse". We'd better go and listen to the news. We'll take the radio in there, leave you two to get sorted. Come on, Brian.'

'Oh, right,' said Brian, who was reluctant to leave the conversation. 'Great to meet you, Bea. Good luck!' He shook her hand, then winked at me. 'And good luck to you too, mate!'

'This is awful,' I said, when they were safely out of the room. 'What have you got yourself into? What have you got me into?'

'It'll be all right,' she said.

'You told me this man is a gangster. And you've stolen his priceless artworks!'

'Well, I didn't actually say that he's a gangster. He knows some pretty dubious-looking people.'

'Well, is he or isn't he?'

'Probably not, but he's still a mean bastard, and I still need help.'

'You shouldn't have taken those things.'

'Yes, I should. I don't feel any conscience about that at all.'

'But … look, you can't keep running away from him. If you're going to give them back … you are going to give them back?'

'What do you think I am, a thief?'

'He probably thinks you're a thief. If you try and get money from him for giving them back, that means you're only a blackmailer.'

'I'm still officially his wife, for God's sake.'

'So what does that make me, the co-respondent?'

'Only if I sleep with you.'

'Don't worry, you're not going to. You'll have to get in contact with him.'

'I don't want to see him again.'

'You'll have to. You have to get this sorted out.'

'Stop panicking, Nigel.'

'I'm not panicking for no reason. Didn't you think this through at all?'

'No, I panicked through a lot of it. I've been under a lot of stress.'

'You can't have been panicking all the time or you wouldn't have thought to hide the loot. And don't tell me where it is, I don't want to know.'

'I have had some lucid moments. I knew you were the kind of sensible, solid person, who would know how to help me.'

'Oh yes, very likely! Well, I'm telling you what to do. Contact Rich, say you're sorry, give him back his things, and see a lawyer about organizing the divorce. You do want a divorce?'

'Haven't you been listening to a word I've been saying? I hate the man.'

'I don't trust you, Bea. I'm sorry, I just don't trust you.'

'Well, I'll be gone in the morning. You can just wash your hands of me and abandon me to my fate.'

I gave her my bed and spent a fairly uncomfortable night on the sofa. The next morning I knocked on the bedroom door, took her in some coffee, said goodbye, told her to keep in touch, wished her luck, and asked her to drop the front door key through the letterbox when she left. She sat up in the bed with her shoulders bare, yawning and nodding vaguely in response. As I went out to go to work, she looked to be settling down again to go back to sleep.

I suppose I was not entirely surprised that evening to come home and find she was still there. In fact, she and Steve and Brian were all waiting for me in some excitement. Bea was sitting on the sofa in my dressing gown, smoking a cigarette.

'I took your advice,' she said.

'Yes,' I said. 'Hello again.'

'I'm sorry, I thought you'd want to be in on this. It *was* your idea, after all. I rang the hotel. I spoke to Rich. His lawyer's coming round here this evening to sort things out.'

'Round here? When?'

'In about half an hour.'

I suppose I must have been a pretty domesticated creature already by then because though my first thought was 'God almighty, Bea!'; my second thought was 'and this place is in such a mess'.

'Why here of all places?'

'It's my territory. Also I thought you and Steve and Brian would be here, in case there's any trouble. They've said they don't mind.'

'I've got the pickaxe handle handy,' said Brian.

'Also I'm pretty sure Rich wants it all kept quiet.'

'Bea …!'

'I know it's a bit of a liberty. But it'll get it settled quickly. I've got to get at my clothes for one thing. I put some things through your washing machine. Do you mind sorting things out a bit, while I get dressed?'

'I hope you know what you're doing.'

'Yesterday was panic day. Now I'm in charge again. Just give me a few minutes.'

She disappeared back into my bedroom. I emptied the ashtray and tidied round a bit in an agitated fashion, still thinking 'of all the gin joints in all the world' etc.

'Have you known her long?' asked Steve.

'Yes and no. We were sort of friends at university. I hadn't seen her for years till she popped up yesterday.'

'You're a good man to help her out with all this — or are you casting your bread on the waters, so to speak?'

'Steve, this is … Let's just say I'm not the first man she's got into a scrape. And there's no bread, no water, believe me.'

'I wouldn't mind casting my bread on her waters,' said Brian.

'You keep your mouth shut while the lawyer's here,' said his father. 'This is serious.'

I pushed back the sofa and brought the dining table further out into the middle of the room, assuming it might be needed if there was any negotiating to be done. Bea came back into the room, and, on the dot of seven o'clock the doorbell rang.

'Mr Anderson?'

'Yes.'

'I'm Antonio Perry, Mr Guildersleeve's representative. This is my associate, Mr Brentano. May we come in?'

Perry was, I'm pretty sure, the man who had been standing with Rich Guildersleeve on the day before. Brentano was a heavily built man in a dark suit, who said virtually nothing throughout the whole proceedings. They both carried briefcases.

I ushered them into the living room. Bea was seated in the centre of the sofa in her smart outfit with her legs together and at a slight angle, smoking another cigarette, and looking as much the poised, sophisticated young society woman as was possible in those ordinary surroundings with two burly coalminers at her back. She didn't get up.

'Mrs Guildersleeve.'

'Hi, Antonio!'

'And these gentlemen?'

'They're staying with me. Mr Philpott, senior and Mr Philpott, junior.' I said.

'I must stress, gentlemen, that everything that passes here must be kept in the strictest confidence. Any breach of confidence will entail immediate recourse to legal sanctions and the rescinding of any agreements reached. In other words, gentlemen, no newspapers or we sue. Do I make myself clear?'

'They understand English, Antonio; they are English.'

'Bloody right!'

'Shush!'

'Then let's get down to business.'

Perry gestured towards the table; Bea gestured him towards an armchair placed opposite the sofa. After a momentary hesitation he sat down, Brentano sat in the other armchair and I sat at the table.

'You won't mind if we tape this conversation for Mr Guildersleeve's benefit?' Perry produced a small tape recorder from his briefcase and perched it on the arm of chair.

'Go ahead,' said Bea. 'So long as you don't mind if I tape it too. Nigel, can you do that for me?'

It took me a second to catch up with that. I fiddled around a bit, found a blank cassette, inserted it in my stereo, plugged in the microphone, and for want of anywhere suitable to place it, sat holding it and pointing it at the main participants. I remembered, finally, to switch the machine on.

'Conversation held on Thursday June 15th 1984 in London at the apartment of Mr Nigel Anderson, those present: Antonio B. Perry Junior representing Mr Richard Guildersleeve, Mrs Beatrice Patricia Guildersleeve, Mr Nigel Anderson, who will identify himself now …' He looked at me pointedly.

'What? Do you want me to say something? Hello!'

'And …' He got Steve and Brian to say their names for the benefit of the tape recorder, which they did rather reluctantly.

'What about him?' asked Brian, pointing at Brentano

'Mr Guildersleeve knows Mr Brentano.'

'But we don't,' pointed out Bea. 'Will you say something, please?' She smiled sweetly at him.

Brentano looked at Perry, then said gruffly 'Henry Brentano.'

'Mrs Guildersleeve, I'll come onto the state of relations between you and Mr Guildersleeve in a moment. First, Mr Guildersleeve is very concerned about the removal of certain items of property from his apartment in New York City. Are you in possession of those items?'

'I know where they are.'

'Are you in possession of them?'

'They're in safe keeping.'

'Are they in England?'

'Yes.'

'I have to remind you, Mrs Guildersleeve, that the removal of Mr Guildersleeve's property …'

'Antonio, can we cut the crap, please? I haven't stolen them; he can have them back. What else does he want?'

'He wants a divorce.'

'So do I. On what terms?'

'On the terms specified in your marriage contract. I have a copy here.'

'I think he can afford to be a little bit more generous than that, don't you?'

'Mrs Guildersleeve, I have to remind you that the removal of your husband's property could be the subject of a criminal investigation.'

'Oh, sure. A wife takes some jewellery with her on a trip to London, even without her husband's say-so. Is that so terrible? Come on, Antonio.'

'The Guildersleeve miniature?'

'I might have wanted to wear it if I was asked to Buckingham Palace. You know I have a friend ... in fact, you know him too, don't you? Saul Bensusan, the guy who writes for the *New York Times*. He is so interested in my husband's business affairs ...'

'Can we get serious here, Mrs Guildersleeve?'

'I am perfectly serious, Antonio. I just want to save dear Richard any embarrassment. Now, can we cut to the deal?'

'Divorce on the original terms, you return the items, and the matter goes no further.'

'No, I'm sorry, no deal.'

'As your legal adviser ...'

'Sorry, Antonio, as my former legal adviser. In the circumstances, I think I need someone who's more on my side, don't you?'

'OK, Mrs Guildersleeve, you get yourself a lawyer, and you come and see us again. Make sure it's a criminal lawyer.' He made a move as if he was going to pack the papers back into his briefcase and leave.

'On the other hand, I might simply go around to the Peruvian embassy in London. Those stones have such a fascinating history. ... Could I have a light, please, Antonio?'

I was amazed at how cool she remained throughout all this. Steve, Brian, and I, looking on riveted, had no idea whether it was simply a game of bluff, or whether we should expect a visit from a posse of police and the Peruvian cultural attaché the next day.

On her second and longer visit to the US, Bea had not simply got the accent and idiom off to a T, but she seemed to have modulated her native English effrontery into genuine all-American chutzpah. Perry seemed to appreciate the performance because he smiled slightly as he leant forward to light her cigarette — but while the tape was running he remained strictly formal.

'To return to the subject of divorce' he went on, giving up the pretence of being about to leave. 'Mrs Guildersleeve, are you having relations with any of these gentlemen?'

'What are you trying to do, get me for having sex with a miner?'

I laughed. Perry looked blank. I explained.

'I was thinking more of Mr Anderson here.'

'Mr Anderson is a dear friend of mine of very long standing, like Mr Bensusan, very like Mr Bensusan in fact. There's no mileage in that. He is kindly letting me use his flat as a base because I have no money. Richard, as I'm sure you know, has stopped all my credit cards, and you surely don't expect me to stay with him in the Dorchester when he's threatening me with prosecution. Now, can we come to some arrangement, please? I'm sure Richard can't bear to be parted from his stones for much longer.'

'All right. Mrs Guildersleeve, I am empowered to offer you a divorce settlement double the one specified in the contract on condition that you return Mr Guildersleeve's property immediately and agree to make no further claims on him.'

'What about my things?'

'You can collect your personal effects from the hotel lobby tomorrow morning. Anything of yours that's still in America, you can collect when you come over for the divorce. Now will you give me the ...'

'And my expenses — you can't expect me to go on sponging off Nigel.'

'I am also empowered to give you twenty thousand British pounds for your maintenance until the divorce is finalized. Mr Brentano, will you show Mrs Guildersleeve the cash?'

Brentano opened his briefcase and displayed a large clear-plastic envelope containing an enormous number of notes. Jaws dropped amongst the simple folk.

'I guess you'll be wanting this then,' said Bea. 'Would you hand me my bag, Nigel.'

I passed her her bag. She took out a small slip of paper and handed it to Perry.

'What's this?'

'It's a ticket for the left-luggage office at Paddington station.'

'Jesus, Bea, are you crazy? This stuff is ...' He recollected himself. 'If you'd just sign this receipt ... and this agreement ... both copies, please'. He passed two documents across to Bea, who signed with a big flourish. Brentano and I signed as witnesses to her signature. 'This conversation terminated at seven twenty three.' He said and switched off his tape recorder, motioning to me to do the same.

'Jesus, Bea! You left the Guildersleeve miniature at the train station?'

'Have you ever heard of a check-room heist, Antonio?'

He laughed at that, unbending considerably now that the business was over and he was no longer being recorded.

'Would you like a drink or anything?' I asked, since things seemed to be getting more amicable.

'No thanks,' said Perry. 'We've got to go and pick up this stuff. It'd better be there, or there'll be big trouble.'

'It's there. The invitation to the Palace never came.'

'Bea, you really are one crazy bitch, you know that?' He stood up to go. 'Take care' he said holding out his hand, 'I mean that, as your former legal adviser, take good care and be careful. I'll see you in court maybe; send me your address, as soon as you have one. I'll let you know where and when.'

'Sure, thanks, Antonio.'

I showed the two Americans out. Perry turned to me as he left, shook hands, and said: 'She's a very smart woman, very smart. You take care too, Mr Anderson. If you weren't a faggot, this could have been a whole lot more complicated.'

The jaw of one of the simple folk dropped again. Back in the living room, Bea punched the air and gave the others each a big hug.

5

Bea treated us all out to a slap-up meal that evening, and ceremonially paid me back the ten pounds. Normal life resumed more or less after that. I had to work on the Friday and to go home on the Saturday for my mother's birthday, as I had promised I would. When I arrived back on Sunday, Steve and Brian were preparing to leave too. They had been watching the television reports of the 'Battle of Orgreave', the most serious clash between miners' pickets and police at a coking plant near Rotherham, and had decided it was time to head for home. They told me that they had helped Bea collect her stuff from the Dorchester and that, in return, she'd gone out collecting with them for the rest of the day and added a good handful of notes of her own to the kitty. Then she'd phoned her parents in Wiltshire and gone to take some of her stuff back to their place. They said that staying in London with me had given them some idea how the other half lived, but that Bea was from another fraction entirely. They wished me luck. I said they needed the luck more than I did. Steve said they'd 'eat grass' before they went back to work on the Coal Board's terms. I hope it didn't come to that.

Bea had left two large suitcases in my flat with a note to say she'd come back and collect them some time, but leaving no address. I put them into the spare bedroom after Steve and Brian left. She had, incidentally, explained Perry's parting reference to a 'faggot'. The man she knew who worked for the *New York Times* was gay. She was pretty pleased with herself for thinking of connecting me with him — in fact she was pretty pleased with the whole way she had handled the situation and the way it had turned out. As well she might be, I suppose. Though perhaps there had been an additional dimension to the conversation that was not wholly apparent at the time. She did give it as her opinion at one point during the celebratory dinner that the secret of a happy marriage, and a happy divorce, was to be very nice to one's husband's attorney.

The whole incident did bring home to me afresh how very, very boring the normal routine of my life had become, and when everyone had gone, the flat seemed very empty.

* * *

The one other noteworthy incident of that summer in my personal world was the birth of my sister-in-law Maisie's baby — a little boy.

I drove up to Lincolnshire with my parents a few days after the event. I no longer had transport of my own. When the Citroen had bitten the dust, there seemed little point in replacing it if I was going to be living in London. The only disadvantage was that I often ended up being driven by my father — who seemed to find an outlet for the aggression that accrued underneath the surface of his regular routine of work and domesticity by driving like a maniac and swearing and gesturing wildly at other motorists who got in his way.

Even before we left home, my mother had begun voicing her anxieties about how a baby could possibly survive and thrive in an environment where the wildlife enjoyed such equality with humanity that it was common to find dog bones buried between the cushions of the old sofa, cats feeding on the sideboard and occasionally invading the dinner table, and parrot droppings almost everywhere. Her frettings increased, the nearer we came to our destination. They ceased, thankfully, when we arrived to a vision of Maisie sitting cross-legged on an old rug in the garden, feeding the baby, while Dave held an umbrella over her to keep off the sun and the two dogs lay stretched out on their bellies with their heads on their front legs looking on. This little nativity scene was broken by the dogs leaping up and barking and carrying on as soon as we got out of the car, but it was evident that, hygiene or no hygiene, everything was basically fine. And once tranquillity was restored, and the three additional baby worshippers were accommodated on kitchen chairs brought out from the house, it seemed that happiness was very easy, in fact. All you needed was a little house and a little piece of ground, another adult to love and, if possible, a baby to be the centre of everything. The look of bliss on Maisie's face said it all.

When little Benedict Arthur (Benedict [Ben], because they liked it, Arthur after Scargill) had finished feeding, he was passed around for everyone to hold, Dave, ever solicitous, going from one baby holder to the other with his umbrella. When my mother passed him on to me — imparting a few lessons in the correct way to cradle an infant in the process — I was amazed at quite how tiny he was, how light, how seemingly fragile. He slept, making slight sucking motions with his mouth and wiggling the fingers of one hand in a haphazard way. He looked, even then, a lot like his mother. He was effortlessly adorable.

I handed him back to Maisie, and my mother asked whether the birth had been easy, perhaps regretting that she had done so when Maisie then launched into a very detailed and gynaecologically explicit account of everything from the first contractions and the breaking of the waters to the delivery of the afterbirth.

Later, in the evening, Dave took father and me to the pub — a fairly rare gathering of the male members of my family. We discussed the strike. Dave was still sanguine about the outcome from the miners' point of view. 'And what,' my father asked, 'will happen to the Labour Party if Arthur Scargill brings down the Tory government?' 'It'll become a proper socialist party at last and we might get a people's government in this country for once,' Dave asserted. 'Never!' retorted my father and a lengthy argument ensued. I had got used to regarding my father as a presence in the household and in my life rather than an active participant. It came almost as a shock to hear him arguing his point passionately with Dave — but then he was always closer to Dave than he was to me. Even though they disagreed on most subjects, they could talk to one another. I resolved to try and establish closer contacts with him.

It is also amazing to think now that, in the mid-1980s, many people thought the ideological struggle between the East and West was still at least evenly balanced and would not have been surprised if Marxist-Leninism had emerged on top. And if the prospect of world domination by a bunch of killjoy ideologues and gulag supervisors in ill-fitting suits was distinctly uninviting, then the notion that Western civilization and values might owe their survival or predominance to Ronald Reagan and Margaret Thatcher was not, to the liberal mind, a source of great comfort either. Nevertheless, on the credit side, we had got to 1984 and the clocks were not yet striking thirteen.

On that Sunday, as we were heading south again in the car, my mother waxed lyrical about little Ben and praised Maisie for her basic maternal skills and attitude, though she was still worried about bringing up a child in 'all that chaos', as she put it. Then she turned her attention to me.

'I wish you were settled, darling. You'll be thirty next April.'

'I know, Mum.'

'It was such a pity it didn't work out with Hilary. She was such a nice girl. I was absolutely certain you were going to get married — George, watch that man, he's trying to cut in!'

My father accelerated and bore down on the cutter-in with his horn blaring.

'I liked her so much. I cried and cried when you told me it was all off. I can't think what possessed her. You were so much in love, the pair of you. It brightened everything when you were there. Oh dear, if I go on thinking about it, I'll set myself off again. What happened about that girl from America?'

'I don't know. I expect she's gone back to sort out her divorce.'

'You let people take advantage of you, you know.'

'I was helping out a friend.'

'She could have got you into serious trouble. It was such an extraordinary thing to do. I don't understand … Anyway, there must be someone in a big place like London. I'd hate to think of you becoming a maiden uncle. You were made to have children. I can see it from the way you were with little Ben, bless him. You can tell when people pick up a baby whether they'd like to have one of their own or not.'

'Mum, I am only twenty-nine. I'm not permanently on the shelf yet.'

'But it's worrying when you get to that age and there's no-one even in sight. The girl from America — even though she's divorced …'

'She's just a friend.'

'She must think something of you to go to you when she's in trouble.'

'It wasn't like that. I told you, she ran into me in Liberty's. It was any port in a storm. Besides …'

'Besides what?'

'She's not my type.'

'I know. Hilary was your type.'

'Please don't go on about Hilary!'

'Yes. I'm sorry. I love you so much, I worry. I'm sorry. — George, we should have turned left there!'

* * *

It would have pleased my mother had she known that, several months later, having just passed the dreaded thirtieth milestone and as the spare man at a colleague's dinner party, I seemed to hit it off well enough with the spare woman for whose sake I had been invited to suggest that we might go out for a drink or even dinner together.

Her name was Jill. She was in her mid-thirties, recently divorced, with a six-year-old daughter called Kate. She worked for a bank in the City, which— or at least this was the impression she gave — was otherwise staffed mainly by incompetents. She lived in a medium-sized terraced house in Islington with a French au pair called Monique to help look after Kate — I got the impression that Monique did not rate very high on the scale of competence either (and was later able to find out why!). When I mentioned the 'Great Business Minds of the Century' project, which it had fallen to my lot to co-ordinate, she pricked up her ears and was, I think, the first person I had come across outside work who had heard of any of the great minds in question. Not that she was terribly complimentary about them. Her critical tendencies apart, she came across as a very lively, very organized and very efficient person. I assumed she had to be to cope with being a single mother with a demanding and responsible job; I also assumed she was perhaps justifiably frustrated by being under-recognized and under-rewarded at work as a result of anti-female prejudice.

What else can I remember about her? She had a big nose, brown eyes, and wore her hair very short. She liked classical music — that was one of the main things we had in common. She was attractive, but in a rather willed sort of way — that is, there was a sharpness, a competitiveness, a drivenness even about most things she did. She presented herself always, rather than simply being herself. I said that we hit it off well, but it would perhaps be more accurate to say that she homed in on me, gave me the works, left me feeling somewhat exercised but basically flattered to be the object of her attentions, and indicated that she would like to take things a bit further, a suggestion I was happy to pick up and run with, especially in my current lonely condition.

We met for a drink, we went out to dinner and got on quite well, I asked her to go with me to a concert at the Festival Hall. After the concert, she invited me to go home with her. To be brutally honest, one main, probably the main source of attraction was that neither of us had had sex for a considerable time. The taxi ride seemed interminable. After the briefest exchange of courtesies with the au pair, we tiptoed frantically upstairs, tore each other's clothes off quietly (all this for the sleeping Kate's benefit), and got down to business with muted gasps and moans. Just before the crucial moment, she whispered hoarsely 'hold it!', rolled over on her side, reached out her arm, opened the drawer of the bedside table, and came back with a condom. In a kind of curtsy to passion she ripped the foil open with her teeth, and with a deftness born of feverish desire or past practice managed to slip it on me and slip me inside herself more or less in one movement. Kate or no Kate, she erupted in one full-volume cry and we both sank back exhausted. Ease after toil, port after stormy seas, sex after abstinence does greatly please.

* * *

It was a new experience, after making a couple more contributions to the health of the condom industry, to sit at the breakfast table on a Saturday morning being sized up by the quizzical looks and questions of a six-year-old.

'Are you Mummy's new fancy man?'

'Kate!'

'Daddy's always asking "has Mummy got a new fancy man?". Is that what he is?'

'He's got a name. Excuse us, Nigel. Monique, are Kate's things ready?'

'*Quoi? C'est pas samedi.*'

'Monique, please speak English, you're never going to learn if you don't speak it. It is Saturday. Colin's coming at ten o'clock. Would you please … no, I'll do it. Please give Kate a boiled egg. Excuse me, Nigel.'

Jill went upstairs to sort out Kate's things. Monique stood in the kitchen looking as if the concept of boiling an egg was something utterly foreign to her.

'Eggs in the fridge,' said Kate, getting one. 'Saucepan in the cupboard. Water in the tap. *Merde* in the toilet.'

'*Chut!*' said Monique. 'How long to boil an egg?'

'Katter minutes, frog's legs' said Kate climbing back onto her chair.

'I don't think Mummy would like you calling Monique frog's legs, Kate,' I suggested cautiously.

'Why not? She's French.'

'Would you like being called a roast beef?'

'I like roast beef. Frog's legs are yucky. *Are* you mummy's fancy man?'

'That's one way of putting it, I suppose. Listen, Monique is like … well, she's like a guest in your house.'

'A guess?'

'A guest, a friend who comes to stay.'

'No, she's not, she's the O pear — *and* Mummy says she's useless.'

'Monsieur, monsieur, the egg!'

'See!'

'Monsieur, it breaks, it goes white! *Ah merde!*'

I rescued what was left of the egg from the white web floating in the saucepan — and put another one to boil — because broken eggs were yucky — and cut some soldiers. Monique sat down at the table and unthinkingly pulled out a cigarette.

'Mummy, she's smoking!'

Monique hastily put the cigarette away again. Jill re-entered in a rush with a small grip and a large teddy bear, looked at me standing at the stove, looked at Monique sitting at the table, and hit the roof.

'Monique for God's sake, that's *your* job. Why are you so bloody useless? Can't you do the simplest things? I'm paying you to look after Kate not to sit on your backside in the kitchen. And I told you strictly no smoking in the house.'

'I do not smoke,' said Monique sullenly.

'Jill,' I said, 'it's OK. Boiling eggs is a dying art. Here, Kate, it's ready.'

'Nigel, let me handle things, please. Kate, do you want this?'

'No.'

'Then go upstairs and wash your hands and face ready for when Daddy gets here.'

'They're clean.'

'Monique, make yourself useful for once, take her up and make sure she has a wash. Now, please!'

Monique hauled the unwilling Kate off upstairs. Jill paced up and down the kitchen.

'The last one I had was so good. She was Spanish. God, I wish she could have stayed. This one is worse than useless. I'll have to get rid of her. I'll ring the agency on Monday.'

I put my hand on her shoulder in what was intended to be a comforting way. She flinched.

'Don't, please. I had it all planned. She doesn't even know what day of the week it is! She ruins everything. I'll get rid of her on Monday. There's Colin. Kate! Monique!'

She picked up the grip and the teddy and went out to answer the door. I sat down and ate the egg. Nobody had actually offered me anything to eat, and it seemed a shame to waste it.

Jill returned after a few moments and sat down. 'Just give me a few minutes,' she said. 'Every time I see him, I just feel the rage boiling up inside me. Give me a moment to calm down.'

I endeavoured to finish the egg as unobtrusively as possible, while she sat with her hands clenched together staring fixedly at the grain in the stripped-pine table and breathing deeply.

None of this seemed terribly promising, in contrast to the pleasures of the night before. After a little while, she regained her composure sufficiently to ask: 'Are you free today? Would you like to take me somewhere?'

I said I hadn't got anything planned and asked where she would like to go.

'Anywhere just to get away from all this. What about the country? Drive me out to the country and let's go for a walk somewhere and have a drink in a pub.'

I explained that this was fine by me, except that I hadn't got a car.

'God, that's a new excuse!'

I protested that it wasn't an excuse but the unfortunate fact. Still, that needn't be a problem. What about a boat ride down the Thames instead?

'I want to get out of London. We'll take my car. You can drive. You *can* drive, can't you?'

I said I could. I suggested, slightly diffidently, that I'd be glad of the chance to call in at the flat on the way just to change quickly. She agreed to that with only a hint of grudgingness, gave instructions to Monique not on any account to leave the house without locking all the doors and windows and setting the burglar alarm, tossed me a set of car keys, and led the way to a row of garages across the street.

Her car was a sleek, virtually brand new BMW, the sort of machine anyone would theoretically give their eye teeth to drive, except, perhaps, someone who was acutely conscious of being surrounded by many thousands of pounds' worth of polished metal and sophisticated engineering, and of being under the direct eye of its critical owner. I made my way cautiously out to Crouch End, only stalling the car once, and beginning, I felt, to get the feel of it.

My flat seemed small and dowdy in comparison to Jill's stylish and interestingly coloured interiors. I left her inspecting the living room and dashed off to freshen up and change into something more suitable for walking in the country. When I emerged, she had put a record on the stereo and was sitting on the sofa drumming her fingers on the arm.

'Your answering machine's flashing,' she said.

'Is it? It's probably my mother.'

'Aren't you going to find out?'

I shrugged my shoulders and pressed the button.

'Hi,' said Bea's voice. 'I'm back. Where are you, you boring man? Do you want to hear the end of the story? Of course you do. I'm a free woman, I'm a rich woman, and I'm a reformed woman. Especially the latter. No more fun and games for this baby. Want to hear more? Of course you do. Call me on …' Then she gave a phone number and rang off.

'You said you were unattached,' said Jill.

'I am …'

'Hello, Nigel, this is your mother. I hope I'm doing this right. Please ring me over the weekend. Your father's not feeling very well again, but he won't go to the doctor. Everything else is all right. I'm putting the phone down now. Goodbye.' (My mother didn't like talking to the machine and didn't trust it.)

'… She's just a friend of mine from university. I helped her out a while back …'

'It's me again. Have you still got those suitcases? You sweet, dependable boy, you. I'm starting my life afresh. It's a blank page. Do you want to be the first name written on it? Of course you do. Call me soon. Mwa!'

The message ended with a big kissing noise. The machine announced that it had no more messages and rewound itself.

'Hadn't you better phone her?' asked Jill frostily, getting up from the sofa.

'There's no rush. I'll ring her later, or tomorrow. I haven't seen her for months.'

'Nigel, I really am not interested in being someone's bit on the side. Can I have my car keys, please.'

'You aren't … I told you the truth when I said I was unattached. Bea is just someone who irrupts into my life from time to time. I'm not sleeping with her. I have never slept with her. I'm not even sure it's right to say we're friends.'

'That's not how it sounds. Give me my keys, please.'

'It's a wind-up. I don't even know what she's talking about — except she's just divorced her husband. It's nothing.'

'Give me my fucking keys!'

I handed her the keys. She flounced out of the flat. I followed her out, knowing that it was useless and undignified to keep on protesting, but still bemused by the storm that had broken about my ears and, even though it was clear that the relationship was a non-starter, mortified that it should have ended so badly and abruptly.

'You're just like every other fucking man on this fucking planet,' she said for the benefit of any passers-by within earshot, got into the car and drove away with a spectacular screech of tyres.

6

Obviously, I wasn't right for her either.

I spent the rest of the day, after calling my mother back, mooching around the flat feeling dissatisfied with my life, trying to decide what to do about it, and considering what I ought to do about Bea.

On the question of the state of my life in general, my assessment was pretty bleak. I had no close friends — that was the worst thing. Whether this was a result of living in the big anonymous city, a product of the long-lasting gloom and negativity that had befallen me after the break-up with Hilary, a manifestation of some deficiency in my character, or simply bad luck, I could not determine — but it made little difference in any case. There was no-one, male or female, whom I could call on at that time for a chat about things or for the boost that comes from simply being in the company of someone who knows you and likes you and is used to sharing experiences with you.

It seemed a symptom of a deeper lack of direction that I should be dependent for human contact and interest on chance encounters — like having a pair of striking miners sent to stay with me, like being latched onto by Bea, like being seized on by Jill as a temporary and inadequate outlet for her frustrations. I was living in the passive voice. I was not in control — not that I imagined that being in complete control of my existence was a realistic prospect or necessarily a desirable thing — but a greater measure of control was surely desirable. If, for example, I had had the kind of political commitment that my brother had and had actively gone out looking for a way to show support for the miners' cause rather than agreeing to let Steve and Brian stay with me, that would have put a completely different complexion on the experience. It would have grown out of something that I was actively engaged in. Perhaps control was the wrong word. Perhaps active engagement was the more fruitful concept. I was not actively engaged in life to a sufficient extent.

And this would explain, perhaps, why I was dissatisfied at work. Since I was facing facts, I ought not, I felt, to shy away from this one. What was I getting out of my job apart from a monthly salary cheque and the ability to say 'I work in publishing'? Precious little was the answer. I was doing my job competently enough, I was working hard, I was on good terms with the people I worked with, and I seemed to be reasonably well regarded by the management, but what did that amount to? Why had I gone into publishing? Because it had to do with what I was good at, trained for, and interested in. I was a words person, a literary gent, a lover of English literature. If I was not actively contributing to the progress of English of literature — and I did not imagine that I possessed any worthwhile writing talent — at least I should be helping to bring a new age of English literature to birth. And if that seemed too grand an ambition, then at least I should be in contact, and exchanging ideas, with people who were writing about things that meant something to me, not badgering academics and retired captains of industry to get them to produce their copy on schedule and tinkering with their leaden prose when they finally delivered it. I would move on. I would see the first couple of volumes of Great Business Minds through to publication, because it would be a bad move to jump ship in the middle of the first major project that had been entrusted to me — unless I was headhunted, of course ... Well, anyway. As soon as the series was properly launched, I would look for something that was more me.

I felt I was getting somewhere. I put on a record of Beethoven's *Eroica* symphony at high volume and strode up and down the room waving my arms and feeling energized and uplifted.

The more immediate question of what to do about Bea was still outstanding, of course. But, drawing on the energy and uplift that was suddenly all around, I was sure I could deal with it.

In any case, was there really a question there at all? What was Bea to me at that stage? A sort of friend. That was it really. We had known each other quite well in our last year at university. She had had a fling with my best friend — a fling that I basically disapproved of and that had occurred at a time when that friend and I were 'breaking up' for want of a better word — and she had dumped him. What did I know about Bea? That she had lots of men and she dumped them. I had witnessed her dumping the tall thin man by the lake, dumping RT outside a seminar room, and dumping her husband in my flat. Common sense said: do not get involved with this woman any more than you currently are because, if you do, she will dump you too. Common sense added: you may have just had an unfortunate experience with Jill, but that was probably down to her rather than to you. You will find someone else, you will also find friends again if you want to and you put yourself about a bit — indeed, if you couple up with someone, finding friends will be a lot easier because people of your age tend to go around in pairs. Common sense concluded: let the woman collect her suitcases and leave it at that, you have got other things to worry about.

On the other hand, Bea was undoubtedly attractive, even glamorous. Life around Bea was not boring, it was precisely the opposite — or appeared to be. Bea seemed to like me; we seemed to be on the same wavelength. Perhaps it was a shared literary interest; perhaps we shared a particular sense of humour. And there was one rather unusual thing about Bea that occurred to me. She did not appear to have many, or perhaps any, girlfriends. I thought of most of the women I had known — not an enormous list — and it was quite easy to imagine them in a circle of other women. Women needed other women, they were good at boosting and supporting one another, they provided each other with shoulders to cry on, they could talk to one another. True, some of them complained that all-female communities were rife with bitchiness and silliness, and they often seemed to have difficulties getting on with their mothers, but by and large they seemed to have an easy, intimate, and supportive commerce with one another. It was a very enviable thing. But when had I seen Bea hob-nobbing with the rest of the girls? Why, when she was in trouble, had she not got straight on the phone to a girlfriend instead of clutching at me as the proverbial drowning man clutches at a straw? Perhaps she simply didn't know anyone in London. Perhaps she had been in America for so long that she had lost contact with everyone she had known in Britain. On the other hand, perhaps she was utterly man-oriented and man-dependent. Perhaps she made other women jealous. Perhaps they felt she was a predator and a show-off. Hilary had had no time for her, I remembered, but that was hardly surprising given what Bea was 'doing to' Caroline. I wished I had someone to talk these things over with instead of merely revolving them round inside my own head.

Nevertheless, although these speculations were interesting, what bearing did they have on the question in hand? OK, Bea was more than usually man-oriented and depended on her way with men for her social life … she also depended on them for her living, because when had I heard Bea ever mention doing any kind of work, except for waitressing and such like when she was in California trying to get into films …. And — that was it, that was surely it, it had been staring me in the face, but had never occurred to me to think it before — she had married Rich Guildersleeve for his money and the security and the kudos of being a multimillionaire's wife. Of course that's what she had done. But, in that case, she couldn't have the slightest interest in me, could she? Common sense returned to make a closing statement: Bea is flirting with you because she flirts with everyone. She can get another man simply by crooking her finger and beckoning. She will doubtless find someone rich and famous to marry. Don't worry, you're not even in the frame. For God's sake, let her take her suitcases and you get on with your life.

* * *

That was enough thinking and stock-taking for one day. I went for a walk on Hampstead heath in the late afternoon, bought myself a steak and a bottle of decent wine, cooked the steak, drank most of the wine, and sat down for an evening of mindless sloth in front of the television, making a mental note to ring Bea on the Sunday and start my new and better life on the Monday.

I believe I had just dozed off when the phone rang.

'Hello?'

'Ha, you *are* there. I couldn't believe you'd be out two nights in a row. Where were you yesterday?'

'I was out.'

'Are you drunk?'

'I don't think so. I think I fell asleep … wait a minute while I turn the television off.'

I tried to remember what resolution I had come to in respect of Bea.

'Hello, I'm back. Where are you?'

'I am at my parents' in darkest, deepest Wiltshire. Did you get my message?'

'Ye-e-es.'

'Nigel, don't yawn when you're speaking to women or you'll be a sad, sexless bachelor all your life. Were you intrigued?'

I tried to remember what the message had said.

'I think so.'

'Nigel, wake up or sober up, this is important.'

'If it's about the suitcases, they're all right, they're still here.'

'Christ, you are obtuse! I don't need suitcases, I need a new life.'

'Join the club.'

'I mean it. If I sounded frivolous yesterday, it's because I thought you might need cheering up.'

'Why would I need cheering up?'

'Because you're a sad sexless bachelor, who looks as though he needs cheering up.'

'Bea, just tell me what you want done with the suitcases and then bugger off.'

'Bugger the bloody suitcases! ... Nigel? Nigel, are you still there?'

'... Yes.'

'I need your help.'

'So what else is new?'

'Everything's new. Boringness is back in fashion. If you'd seen what I've seen ... Are you listening?'

'Bea can you give me one good reason — even if I could help you — why I should want to, when you keep calling me a sad sexless bachelor and go on about how boring I am.'

'I want to talk to someone who's not my bloody mother.'

'Then try your bloody father!'

'Fuck you, Nigel!'

And she rang off.

I just had time to feel quite pleased with myself for standing up to her, when the phone rang again.

'I'm sorry.'

'Really.'

'No, I am, I'm sorry. I'm a bitch.'

'You said it.'

'Be nice to me, please. All those things I said about being a reformed woman and making a new start, I meant them. I've been in New York. All my friends are dying of AIDS.'

'What?'

'It's the most horrible, unspeakable thing ... I know, knew lots of gays. Saul Bensusan, that guy I told you about who sometimes writes for the *New York Times* ... he hasn't got it, but lots of other people have. The ones that haven't are desperately worried and devastated because the people they know are dying. All the charming, witty, creative people I knew ... Anyway, it's made me think.'

'I'm sorry.'

'I was worried for myself as well.'

'But you were married.'

'Well, I was, but how the hell did I know who Rich had been with, and anyway, I wasn't ... anyway.'

'Can you get yourself ... can you have a test?'

'I've done that. I'm OK, physically. But it doesn't make me feel I want to go on ... you know. And I'm thirty-two. I have to start behaving responsibly some time. That's a sad, sad thing to have to say, isn't it?'

'I suppose so.'

'I'm a sadder and a wiser woman — that's what I should have said yesterday. Also a richer woman, but that doesn't mean very much ... anyway, I have to do something with my life. How are you?'

'I'm OK, a bit lonely, a bit bored, nothing serious.'

'I was only joking when I said ...'

'No, no, it's true, more or less ...' and I gave her an edited account of my encounter with Jill and the part her answering-machine message had played in it.

'She sounds terrible. You weren't worried about going to bed with her?'

'Well, no. I hadn't given it any thought, to be honest, being ... well non-ogamous most of the time. Anyway, strictly condom. So ...'

'I do want to talk things over with someone. Can I come and see you?'

'I've got a busy week coming. I really have. That's not an excuse. And I'm in the middle of trying to sort my life out as well.'

'Are you? Why?'

'I just don't think it's going anywhere — usual thing.'

'Do you fancy a weekend in the country? My father's been away on business, but he's coming back this week … which makes it just about bearable to stay here a little longer. Come down next weekend. Are you free?'

'Being free most of the time is one of the things I'm trying to sort out. I'll come if you want me to.'

'Yes, please. You haven't got a car, have you? Tell me when you're coming and I'll meet you off the train …'

7

I put the phone down puzzled. Had I really been speaking to a new Bea? The thoughts I had been having about her no longer seemed very relevant … but can the leopardess change her spots? Apparently between two phone calls? I decided it was best to keep an open mind and try not to think about it too much.

I had actually been due to go home on the weekend in question. I rang my mother to postpone. She was still worried about my father. He had taken some days off work, but was still refusing to go to the doctor. Would I speak to him, she asked. She was gone a long time from the phone and I imagined her having to cajole or bully him to come and talk to me — he didn't like talking on the phone particularly. I could hear him grumbling and her urging him as he came out of the living room into the hall where the telephone was.

'Hello?'

'Dad, how are you?'

'I'm fine.'

'Mum says you haven't been well.'

'She fusses. I'm not getting any younger, that's all.'

'But didn't you ought to go and see the doctor?'

'No.'

'Just for a check-up.'

'No.'

'It can't do any harm.'

'It won't do any good.'

'Well, to please Mum — to please me.'

'Nigel, you're getting like your mother, don't fuss. I'm fine. Are you going away for the weekend next week?'

'Yes, but …'

'Have a good time. Bye.'

He laid the receiver down and shuffled off. My mother picked it up again.

'What am I going to do with him?'

'Is he any better?'

'He says he is. He's going back to work tomorrow.'

'What exactly's wrong?'

'It's his stomach. He says it's just indigestion. But he gets terrible pains some times and he comes home from work looking absolutely washed out. It's not right. I wish he'd retire early. He's only got four more years to go anyway and, you know your father, he's always been very careful. But he won't.' She dropped her voice to a whisper. 'Do you think it could be cancer?'

'No. Surely …'

'That's what's worrying me.'

'If he won't go to the doctor … Have you got Dave to talk to him?'

'He won't listen to anyone.'

'He's more likely to listen to Dave than to me. We just have to keep on at him, until he goes. Do you want me to cancel next weekend?'

'No, no. Don't be silly. And don't worry too much. I probably am fussing. Anyway, tell me where you're going …'

* * *

It was a busy week, so I didn't have too much time to think either about Bea or the situation at home. I did manage, as part of the general life-modernization plan, to slip out and buy myself a few clothes, conscious that, apart from anything else, I should be meeting Bea's parents for the first time — of whom I knew absolutely nothing, but whom I assumed to be fairly grand. She obviously had not issued from a country cottage.

I got out of the train on the Saturday morning in a small Wiltshire town, carrying three suitcases — two of Bea's, which weighed a ton, and one of mine, which was also heavier than it need have been because I had no idea what sort of activities I might be called on to participate in over a May weekend.

There was nobody to meet me. The train was more or less on time. I waited on the forecourt looking at my watch, reminding myself that I had phoned ahead and given the time and that Bea had promised she would meet me, but wondering whether I ought to phone again or take a taxi. Eventually a mud-splashed Range Rover tore onto the forecourt and Bea jumped out.

'Sorry,' she said, 'another row. God, I have to get out of here.' She took both my hands in hers. 'Pleased to see me?'

'Yes,' I said.

'Good,' she said and leaned forward and kissed me on the lips. 'All right, back to Hell Hall. You look neat.'

'Thanks,' I said. 'You look wonderful.' She was in an old pair of jeans, a roll-neck sweater, and a Barbour coat. She had her hair gathered on top of her head and an old cap of her father's on. More significantly, in my eyes, she was wearing the Liberty scarf I had bought her as a disguise around her neck. In the intervals between our scattered meetings, I seemed to forget how extremely attractive she was.

'This is my blending-in gear. You should see me in some of the frocks I bought in New York.'

As we were driving back through country lanes, she filled me in on her parents. Her father was ex-army, now a director of an international company based in Swindon. He travelled a lot, because it was preferable to spending time in an office in Swindon and, no doubt, to spending time at home. Bea's mother trained dogs. The worse relations got between her and her husband, the more 'doggy' she became, according to Bea. They had separate bedrooms and frequent rows. This morning's row had been about the gas bill. Bea got on with her father most of the time, but didn't get on with her mother.

'I'm sorry to bring you into all this. But it is beautiful down here. I love it. And you'll see why I need rescuing again.'

'Bea, you don't really need rescuing. Come on, you're thirty-two, you're your own woman, you've got money.'

'Well, maybe — but it's even nicer to be rescued when you don't need it. This is it. Tread carefully!'

We pulled off the road into a short drive that led up to a large, handsome Georgian house, the 'Old Rectory', to be greeted by two large brown and white spaniels. Bea beeped the horn a couple of times to signify our arrival. Nobody came out.

We went inside.

'Hello, we're back,' Bea called. When there was still no reply, she added, 'Mother's probably out with the dogs. God knows where Father is. I'll show you your room.'

She led the way upstairs and showed me into a large light room overlooking the garden. It contained a large metal bedstead; there were hunting prints on the walls.

'There's my father,' she said, pointing out of the window. Towards the bottom of a long garden a tall, erect-looking man in his sixties dressed in jeans and an old army pullover was throwing twigs and assorted garden rubbish onto a bonfire. As we watched, a woman in green Wellington boots, an old tweed skirt, and a headscarf, came through a gate at the bottom of the garden with two Dobermans and a Jack Russell on leads.

'My mother,' said Bea.

Mrs Williams walked straight up the garden without exchanging a word or a look with her husband, nor did he look up from the bonfire as she went by.

'Oh God! I'll go down and see what's going on. Why don't you slip into something scruffier and come down in a minute.' She led me to the door. 'Your bathroom's there,' she said pointing one way down the corridor, 'my room's there, but … not this time, OK?'

'OK,' I said. It was what I expected, but no longer, I found somewhat to my surprise, what I wanted.

'And remember, you're here for me!'

She kissed me on the cheek and went downstairs calling to her mother.

I sat down on the bed and tried to catch up for a moment. All this affection, was it real? She was being so sweet! Bea Williams, sweet? It had, after all, been 'fuck you, Nigel' only a week ago. Well, that was perhaps incidental, but still … And why me? What had I got to offer? I rooted in my case for the walking clothes I had packed and got changed slowly. And what did I feel for her, apart from lust? I could not deny a certain warming towards her. But … Realizing that I ought not to take too long before putting in an appearance, I used 'my' bathroom quickly, put on a pair of actually brand-new jeans and a sweater, and went down.

'Nigel, how nice to meet you!' said Bea's mother offering her hand. 'I hope you don't mind dogs. Get off, Dickens!' This was to one of the brown-and-white spaniels who was showing an unhealthy interest in my new jeans. 'This one's Dickens, the other one's Thackeray. That was Beatrice's idea. They're ours. Any other dogs you see around the place are just boarders. Dickens, get off. It's just because he likes you. Beatrice, dear, would you see if your father's ready for lunch? You don't mind if we have lunch in the kitchen, do you, Nigel, we're very informal. Sit down, please.'

Bea returned with her father from the garden. I stood up to shake hands.

'What did she say your name was?'

'Nigel … Anderson. How do you do?'

'Won't shake hands, they're dirty.' He went over to the sink to wash them. 'Where are you from?'

'London.'

'Originally?'

'Essex.'

'What Colchester? Chelmsford? I know Colchester, of course.'

'A little place called Roxdon. It's on the Cambridge line, not far from Harlow.'

'What Harlow New Town? Isn't that a God-awful place like Swindon? Anyway, never heard of Roxdon. Country, is it?'

'Yes. Well, not quite like here. Getting quite built up. It's near London.'

'Do you shoot?'

'I'm afraid not.'

'Pity, thought about going out with a gun this afternoon. What about it Bea?'

'We might go along for the walk.'

'I'll bring the dogs,' said Bea's mother.

'I thought the dogs had had a walk.'

'Not Dickens and Thackeray.'

'They don't need you to take them.'

'No, Bill, but we'll come along to keep you company.'

'Come along to spite me more like it. Can you pass the butter …?'

'Nigel, Dad.'

'My wife and I don't get on. I'll tell you now because you're bound to notice. Have you got parents?'

'Er — yes.'

'They all right? Divorced? At each other's throats?'

'All right, I think.'

'Rare these days. Ginny can't wait to dance round my grave, can you, darling?'

'No, darling.'

'You don't object to a bit of guerrilla warfare, do you? Too bad if you do. Has he got boots, Bea? It's pretty muddy up by the copse.'

'Have you got boots?'

'No.'

'You can draw a pair from the cupboard by the back door. I'll just go and get the gun.'

Major Williams — Bea had primed me not to make the mistake of calling him Mr — got up and left the room.

'You mustn't mind my husband, Nigel. The best thing to do is to ignore him. Believe me, I know. I've had years of practice.'

Bea took me to the cupboard by the back door, which was full of rubber boots in different sizes and assorted outdoor gear for casual, ill-equipped guests. I sorted out a pair of Wellingtons that were my size.

'Do I need a jacket?' I asked. 'I've got one upstairs.'

'Not if it's a decent jacket. Put one of these on. And how about a hat? You've got to look the part.' She took a cap off a peg. It was miles too small. 'You have got a big head. Is it brains or is it pride? How I'd like to see inside.' I found myself kissing her again — seriously this time, and being kissed seriously back. She pulled away and laid her finger on my lips. 'You'll make me break all my resolutions,' she said.

Dickens and Thackeray came bounding round the side of the house followed by Mrs Williams. The Major came out with a shotgun crooked over his arm. We headed off down the garden, through the gate, over a lane, and then via a stile onto a footpath along the edge of a field, heading towards a range of low wooded hills in the distance.

The Major and Mrs Williams, of course, would not walk together on principle. Where the path was wide enough for two or more to walk abreast, Bea generally walked beside her father and I walked with her mother. Dickens and Thackeray sprinted to and fro all around us, when they weren't exploring the undergrowth or marking fenceposts.

'How very nice of you to walk with me, Nigel. It's pleasant to have some non-canine company.'

'Not at all. Thank *you* for having me here.'

'It's a pleasure. As you'll have gathered, my husband isn't what you'd call a helpmate or a soulmate … By the way, I meant what I said at lunch. Ignore him. He only does it to intimidate people, especially anyone who looks like a possible suitor for Beatrice.'

'Well, I'm not sure I fall into that category, but I'll do my best not to be intimidated.'

'That's good. You seem to be the sensible type, if you don't mind me saying so.'

'I don't object to being called sensible.'

'Good sense seemed to be a rarity in the chaps Beatrice knocked about with before she was married, but there were so many of them, who am I to say?'

Ahead of us, the Major stopped, pointed across the field, gestured to everyone to keep still and be silent, and brought his gun up to his shoulder. I stopped more or less automatically. Mrs Williams carried on walking.

'Dickens, Thackeray, with me! Come along, Nigel. As I said, ignore him.'

The Major brought his gun down again and gave his wife the evil eye as she passed, whilst I exchanged some comic eye-goggling with Bea. Dickens and Thackeray would obviously have dearly liked to stay and wait by the gun, but they were ordered on. We, that is the dogs, Mrs Williams, and I, crossed the next stile and began to ascend a fairly steep, stony path through trees with a small stream running down the middle of it.

It was quite hard going up the incline and I was glad when we stopped for a breather at the top. Mrs Williams gestured for me to sit down beside her on a large tree stump. Two shots rang out in the distance. The dogs quivered and pricked up their ears, desperate for permission to go off and search for a kill. It was not given.

'That's another poor rabbit gone to meet its maker. I have to say I think better of you, Nigel, for not being a hunting man. Beatrice shoots, you know.'

'I didn't know. It's rather funny to think of Bea with a gun.'

'It's her father, you see. Anything he does, she does. It's the way it's always been and, I suppose, it's the way it always will be. Are you all right? Ready to move on? Do say if you're not, I've got nothing to do all day except walk dogs. It means I'm as fit as a fiddle. I dare say you don't get that much walking in London.'

In a short while we came out of the wood onto the top of the ridge and began to walk along it. There was a fine view over the valley, but no sign of Bea and her father, except for the occasional sound of a shot coming from inside the wood.

'I expect we'll get home before them, I'm sorry to have kept you away from Bea,' Mrs Williams went on.

'Not at all. It's been a lovely walk. What a glorious view this is.'

'It is. There's Hell Hall, I mean our house, the Old Rectory. See! Just to the right of the church spire.' She pointed across the valley. I nodded, hoping I was looking at the right house. 'We all call it Hell Hall. It wouldn't surprise me if the rest of the village does too. Three is a terribly unlucky number. It doesn't divide up properly. There's always an odd one out.'

'Ah, you mean in your family.'

'Yes. Have you got brothers and sisters, Nigel?'

'One brother.'

'I should have had more children. When he was in the army, we were always being moved about. He said one was enough. That was all right for him, of course. She's always been his little girl. They're like that,' she clasped her two hands together, 'and that doesn't leave any room for me.'

'Yes, I can see that's very sad for you. ... My mother's always said she would have liked another child. She's sorry she never had a girl.'

'Is she? Why?'

'She thought she would have been closer to a daughter — you know, woman to woman.'

'Huh! No disrespect to your mother, Nigel. But that is not how it works. Believe me, I know. Thackeray, leave that!'

Thackeray left it. We walked a little further in silence.

'How long have you known my daughter, Nigel?'

'I don't know. I knew her at university. Not very well. The best part of ten years probably, but we've got to know each other better recently.'

'You know about her husband, of course.'

'I never met him. She told me a little about him.'

'He was a very nice man. I liked him. He was very polite and charming, as Americans are. And generous. Bill couldn't stand him, but then he was taking his little girl away for good, as he thought. She gave Richard an awful time.'

'Really? I thought it was rather the other way round.'

'You'd be well advised not to believe everything my daughter tells you, Nigel. I'm her mother, God knows, but truthfulness is not her forte. She was only after his money, of course. Well, he scuppered that little plan rather neatly, and I don't blame him. Then she slept with half New York and ran off with a family heirloom. Need I say more?'

She stood still and looked me straight in the eye. I thought I'd better steer us back to a safer subject. 'As I say, I never met him. I don't know anything about their married life. But generally speaking, I tend to go on the principle that if there's trouble in a marriage it's most likely to be six of one and half a dozen of the other. Anyway, that tower over there sticking up through the trees …'

'You're quite wrong, Nigel. She was entirely to blame.'

'Well, that wasn't the impression I got.'

'Impressions can be deceptive. She led him a dreadful dance. I hope you're not harbouring too many illusions about her. People see the long blonde hair and think she must be an angel. You do know she's had hundreds of men. Her parts must be like old leather by now.'

'I … I think hundreds is perhaps a slight exaggeration.'

'Perhaps you've had hundreds of women too. How should I know, why should I care? But you don't seem that sort of chap. From the age of fifteen, she hasn't been able to keep her hands off anything in trousers. She's now thirty-two. My arithmetic isn't that good, Nigel, but twenty men a year is probably a conservative estimate, work it out for yourself.'

'Mrs Williams …'

'I dare say they're all substitutes for her father, but does that make it any better? Can't keep her knickers on, but doesn't really want a man for anything more than a five-minute roll in the hay. None of them comes up to his standard, you see. As soon as she finds that out, she gets furious with them and dumps them. It's what happens every time. But men can't seem to see past the blonde hair and the gift of the gab. Anyone who takes her on is making a rod for his own back, that's all. I'm sorry to say it, but I'm her mother, I do know what I'm talking about.'

'I'm sorry, but I'm not sure you do.'

She looked at me long and hard. 'I'm disappointed in you, Nigel,' she said. And, calling the two dogs to order, she walked off down the hill.

I was uncertain what to do next — given that it was about three miles back to base and I had only a rough idea where I was. I did not want to hear Bea being slagged off any more, and it seemed ridiculous to follow in Mrs Williams's footsteps at a safe distance, so I elected to try and find my way back by the way we had come, hoping that I might come across Bea and her father somewhere in the woods or fields.

Somehow I missed the path that led down the hill, and when I eventually found my way down to a lane at the bottom of the valley, I set off in the wrong direction until I came across a signpost with the name of the village on it. I trudged back along the lane, deciding to play safe and not attempt to cut across the fields, but the road took a far less direct route, so that it seemed like hours before I got to the village and then I had to ask the way to Hell Hall. I rang the doorbell.

'Where the hell have you been?' asked the Major. 'Bea's out looking for you.'

'I got lost, sorry.'

'Nigel, dear, I thought you were following me,' Mrs Williams sounded full of concern.

'I must have got distracted ... at a critical moment. I'm sorry. Shall I go and find Bea?'

'God, no,' said the Major. 'You'll only get lost again. See to him, Ginny.' He went off towards the back of the house.

'Perhaps, I'd better take these boots off. They're very muddy.'

'Yes, go round to the back and come in that way, if you don't mind. I'll get you a drink. What would you like?'

'Brandy, please ... and soda, if that's OK.'

I must have been looking at her oddly because she went on, 'Is there something else you wanted to say?'

'No,' I replied. And that was the only allusion she made — if indeed it was one — to what had been said at the top of the hill.

As I came around to the back of the house, there was a tremendous bang that sent pigeons shooting up out of the trees and set all the dogs in the village barking, especially the boarder dogs who must have been penned up somewhere near the house. Standing on the back doorstep, the Major lowered his gun, broke it, and removed the spent cartridge. 'That'll bring her back,' he said drily, and went inside again.

8

I concluded that the fact that Bea was not barking mad like both her parents was a tribute to her strength of character.

It was not easy to sleep that night, not so much because of the continual noise from the boarder dogs, but because I was trying to reassess my position vis-à-vis Bea. I was falling for her, that much was obvious, and it was tempting to think that this was the culmination of some gradual, destined process that had been set in train the first time I saw her — which was unlikely because I nearly dropped a briefcase on her from the top of a staircase in the Arts Block and her very first words to me were 'Were you trying to assassinate me?' — or some other time at university or at least the time when she happened upon me in Liberty's. Rationally, this notion was nonsense, but it seemed to hover, beckoning to me to come and take hold of it, to revise any previous version of our history and adopt the romantic one as the true account.

I tried to fight it off by reviving the common-sense approach. I did know Bea. Even if I put her mother's words of the previous day down to some peculiar warping of the mother–daughter relationship and blatant jealousy, she had revealed nothing, really, that I did not know before. I had been warned off her. I had warned myself off her. Her behaviour towards me had changed, but was the change real? I would have said that she was quite possibly falling for me, but how could this be? Only a week ago, I had worked out a rational scenario for what Bea would do now she was back and a free woman. In that scenario, I would have no role or only a very minor one. Now we were exchanging kisses that seemed to promise all sorts of other things. We could end up loving each other, living together … But, what if making up to me was part of some larger plan? Calculatedness was not something I would have attributed to Bea. But, according to her mother, Bea had gone into her marriage with the charming, generous Rich Guildersleeve for purely mercenary motives. She had, moreover, shown herself a pretty shrewd operator in precipitating the divorce and handling the lawyer. But then Antonio Perry ('be very nice to your husband's attorney') was probably included in 'half of New York'. But then again, Bea might have slept with him deliberately because she knew she might need a favour some day. But did that make it any better?

I had to talk to her. I had to sort some of these things out. I had to clear my head before I let myself get too far in. But what was all this about 'getting too far in'. Say that all Bea had in mind was another fling — with me. Would I really turn that down, even though it was not what I really wanted? I wanted a serious, long-term relationship with someone: that was the number-one aim. But if what was on offer was a few weeks or months of passion with a brilliantly attractive and exciting woman, a woman who had had 'hundreds of men' and quite probably possessed a sexual artistry undreamt of by the likes of me ... well, no, actually attested to by my former best friend in the course of slagging off both myself and his workaday lover as impediments to his attaining his proper place in the hierarchy of passionate exalted beings ... then only a fool or a puritan would let the opportunity slip. And I was surely neither of those.

But what was I? And why would she practise those arts on me? What was in it for her? What was the plan?

At three o'clock in the morning, the mind, freewheeling though seeming to follow a logical train of thought, grinds things very small.

It is not easy untangling motivation. We generally divide behaviour into the spontaneous and the calculated, and set the heart against the head. In love it is the involuntary that counts: 'I can't help loving you'; 'I fell'; 'You made me love you'; 'Even so quickly may one catch the plague?'; and thousands more such sayings. If we only could, the implication seems to be, we would carry on with our lives in single blessedness, avoiding the plague, the infection, the burden of obsessively desiring and thinking about someone else.

But that is obvious nonsense. It must be in our basic biological nature to need a mate. 'The world must be peopled'. At a slightly more sophisticated level, most of us must seek, more or less actively, to love and be loved. And that must be true for both sexes, even though, in the traditional language, men pursue and women surrender. But while we're aware of the pro-active element in our own wooing, we tend not to attribute much pro-activity to the person 'pursued'. We certainly seem to flinch from reconstructing the language of love to accommodate its goal-driven aspects. There is a kind of insurance in the old notions and language. Our strong needs make us vulnerable. We desperately need to feel that we are not merely the victims of someone else's agenda, of some kind of plot to take us over body and soul and subjugate us to their whims and fancies or worse. Mutual helplessness in the face of overwhelming attraction is a kind of guarantee of honest intentions on both sides.

So, I wanted to know why Bea had turned to me. I don't think I ever really found out. Given her background, it was likely she might do something odd. Perhaps she wanted to try someone who was totally unlike her father. Perhaps, after her previous history, she just wanted someone soothing, stable, and relatively ordinary. Perhaps, perhaps. I hope she did love me too — at least a little.

* * *

I finally fell asleep in the big iron bed and awoke to find her sitting on the end of it in a dressing gown, loosely tied, looking at me.

'Tea?' she said, pointing to a cup on the bedside. 'It's probably cold, I'm afraid. I didn't think you were ever going to wake up.'

'I'm sorry. I didn't sleep very well.'

'The dogs, I expect.'

'Yes, mainly.' I hitched myself up higher in the bed and tried to get back to full consciousness. 'We must …'

'We must talk.'

'Yes.'

'Seriously.'

'Yes.'

She shuffled a bit closer along the bed, took my hand, and placed it inside her dressing gown and held it against her breast.

'Bea!' I moaned, protestingly, but making no effort to get my hand back.

'I just long so much for you to touch me. It's so stupid. And I'm not supposed to be trying to seduce you. I …' She dropped my hand abruptly, stood up, and turned away.

I scrambled out of bed and took her in my arms. She was crying.

'I can't help it. My whole life's falling apart. I don't know what's happening to me.'

'It's not. It's all right. We'll sort it out.'

'Oh God, this is so stupid. I need you. Please … please.'

I held her tightly in my arms and then kissed her with more intensity than I've ever kissed anyone, as if my whole soul was in my lips.

'It's all right. I love you. It's all right.'

She smiled up at me tearfully. 'Thank God,' she said, and crushed her face into my shoulder.

* * *

There really was a lot to talk about. We borrowed one of the family cars and drove off to Stourhead, the spectacular

National Trust property near Frome, ostensibly to see if the rhododendrons were out. I think they were, but it would probably not have made much difference had we stayed in the car park rather than doing three circuits of the extravagantly pretty lake. 'We stayed in the car park till quarter past one / And now I'm engaged to Miss Joan Hunter Dunn'.

We did not get engaged, but we did clear things up and come to some sort of an understanding and make a plan.

Bea said that she had at first envisaged staying in the US after the divorce, but that going back to New York and seeing so many of her friends in such a parlous state — ill, dying, grief-stricken or fear-stricken — had depressed and frightened her, and she had felt the whole metropolitan hugeness and the colossal, ruthless energy of the place as intolerably oppressive. So she decided to come home, and as soon as she thought about coming back to England, she said, she thought of me. And as soon as she started thinking of me, she couldn't stop. But she had no idea how I really felt about her. She said she wouldn't have blamed me if I hadn't wanted to touch her with a bargepole after the way she had treated me. I said that I wasn't aware that she'd ever treated me badly. Well she had, she insisted, or she felt she had, or she felt, at least, that I must disapprove of her. I was one of the few men who had resisted her charms, after all. 'Aren't I mad, bad, and dangerous to know?' she asked. 'I'm sure that's what my mother told you.'

I admitted that it was, and she then launched into an explanation of the situation between herself and her mother. As she saw it, her mother was insanely jealous of her relationship with her father and, indeed, of almost any close relationships she formed with anybody. Her mother, she said, never lost an opportunity to run her down to her friends, starting with her friends from prep school.

'I'd bring these girls home in the holidays,' she said, 'and my mother would be very nice to them, as sweet as pie.

Then, after a couple of days, she'd start telling them what an unloving, ungrateful, treacherous little brute I was, while at the same time praising them to the skies to me and telling me how perfect they were and how she wished she had a daughter like them instead of a poisonous little reptile like me. And she told me no-one would ever love me, no-one would ever marry me, I'd never have any children. So I set out to prove her wrong, of course. Except that it wasn't simply that. I get on with men. They find me attractive. Going with men was my way of finding out about life and exploring the world. Am I doing the right thing to say this to you?'

'That is … that was the main thing I knew about you.'

'It's the main thing that everyone knows about me, but what everyone thinks about me doesn't matter. What you think about me does.'

'Isn't every new relationship a new start in a way?'

'Well, it is and it isn't. If you go from one person to another, they start to blend in eventually. Some are more important than others, of course. That man from South Africa at university — the one who knocked my teeth out — he was pretty important. But your friend RT wasn't — not very. He was fun, but that was all. There was a man I knew in California before I married Rich who was absolutely wonderful in every way, but he didn't have much money and didn't want to marry me and Rich had money and did. I must be punishing myself by telling you all these things. Thank God you're not jealous. Are you jealous?'

'No, I'm not jealous. But I've just discovered that I love you, and if it turns out that I'm just the next in line, the next one for the blender, then I might as well go and jump in that lake and have done with it.'

'Please, Nigel, it is different. I am different. When I saw you yesterday, I knew I'd done the right thing to come back. I felt I'd come home. I was just desperate to know whether you felt anything for me.'

'Are you fishing for me to say "I love you" again, because I'll do it. It's no hardship.'

'I'm not fishing for you to *say* it, I'm desperate for you to *do* it.'

'But why me? This is what I don't understand. I just have to look at you, I just have to be with you to know that you are the most lovable thing on God's earth.'

'I'm not.'

'You are.'

'I'm not. Seriously, I'm not.'

'You are, I insist. "Earth has not anything to show more fair …"'

'You are so corny. I won't have you after all.'

'Yes you will.'

'No, I won't. Well, weeeell, maybe, if you're very good. I thought this was supposed to be a serious talk.'

'Reassure me. Tell me at least two things, no three things. Tell me three things about me that you really like.'

'Now who's fishing?'

'I am … please, I never get any compliments.'

'I love you because you're you — will that do?'

'Now who's being corny.'

'I don't want to put it into words. Really, I don't want to put it into words. It might unscramble everything. Just depend on it; you are loved. I love you.'

And who wouldn't make do with that?

***

From there we had to go on to make some concrete plans. We sat down on a stone bench beside one of the temples. She couldn't stay with her parents, she said. I said I didn't want her to; I wanted her to come back with me to London, the sooner the better.

'When? Tonight?'

'If you like.'

'Can I? Do you want me to?'

'Why wait?'

'Are you absolutely sure you want me in your life? I suppose I don't have to live with you. If I could stay with you, until I find myself somewhere.'

'Well, I hope you don't ... I mean, all right, let's see how it works out. But I want it to work out.'

'This is very strange. I mean, I didn't invite you down here, expecting you'd take me back with you. I suppose I hoped you would. I'll have to get a job, I suppose.'

'Well, London's the best place.'

'Yes, but I can't do anything.'

'Have you really never had a proper job before?'

'I told you: my life's been bizarre, bizarre, bizarre. I can wait tables.'

'There are hundreds of things you could do. You won't need to do that. Anyway, didn't you tell me you were a rich woman?'

'I was forgetting that. Yes — well — -ish! Look at that!'

She pointed down to the lake. What looked at first sight like a stick in the water or one of the numerous small waterfowl, was in fact the head of a snake. It swam, laboriously swishing its tail but quite fast, across the mouth of the small bay above which we were sitting and disappeared into the reeds.

'I've never seen that before,' said Bea. 'It must mean new things are happening. Anyway snakes are lucky.'

'Not if they bite you. Who says they're lucky?'

'D.H. Lawrence — and the Goon Show. It's my father's favourite joke.' She put on the voice of the Mighty Eccles. '"Put a snake in my bed tonight" "Why?" "It's lucky" "Why's it lucky?" "It's not every snake that sleeps in a bed!" And talking of my father, we'd better go home and tell them I'm leaving.'

9

Informing Bea's parents was a double job. Her mother was out of the house when we arrived back. Bea went to tell her father, who was upstairs in his study. She asked me to fetch down the two suitcases that I had brought the day before and ring for a taxi to take us to the station.

I was on the phone when Mrs Williams came back and overheard me.

'You don't need a taxi, Nigel. Beatrice will take you to the station, unless she's fallen out with you. Has she?'

'No. She's coming with me.'

She stared at me.

'What do you mean?'

'She's coming to stay with me. She's going to live in London.'

'With you? Is that what you think? You bloody fool!'

'I know you don't know me. I don't expect you to like me. But, as it happens, I love her and I'm not a bloody fool.'

'Well, I hope you enjoy misery, Nigel, because you've got a lot of it coming. Excuse me, I've got to feed the dogs. Tell Beatrice I'll expect her when I see her. She always ends up coming back here, you know, when she's ruined some other man's life. I give you three weeks. Goodbye.'

She turned round and went out again.

The Major was slightly less ungenerous in his farewells.

'What's all this about?' he asked as he came down the stairs.

'Bea's coming back to London with me.'

'I know that. You equipped to take on this sort of thing?'

'Equipped?'

'Resources — financial and character-wise, that sort of thing. I don't know you. You look like an average sort of fellow. Are you?'

'It depends what you mean by 'average'. I suppose so. Yes.'

'She's pretty independent-minded, but needs looking after. Not just in bed. Can you do that?'

'I know Bea; she can look after herself.'

'You think so, do you?'

'Yes.'

'I think she needs a fellow with a strong character and a firm hand. You probably think that's old-fashioned rubbish. That's the mistake most of them make. I wouldn't have had you down as a particularly strong character. One piece of advice. Don't let her get bored, and don't try and get pally with her mother.'

'Not much chance of that.'

'You've had the baptism of fire, have you? Well, I suppose you're marginally more promising than the last one anyway. Good luck — er …?'

'Nigel.'

'Yes. Are you ready, Bea?'

'Can someone give me a hand with this case?' Bea called from the top of the stairs. The Major motioned me forward, as if indicating that all this was my responsibility now. I struggled down with another bulging suitcase and Bea followed with a couple of lighter bags. The taxi arrived. Bea gave her father a long hug, shouted goodbye to her mother, and we left.

We didn't talk much in the train back to Waterloo. I was filled with wonder at the speed with which things had developed … and inclined to believe that the suddenness and completeness of the change was a sign of the intrinsic rightness of the new situation. Things had come together because they were meant to. I was also filled with a new sense of responsibility, not wholly prompted by the Major's remarks. I felt responsible for the woman sitting beside me, holding my hand and occasionally pointing out familiar landmarks along the line. Though she was older than me, and better-off, and, I assumed, infinitely more worldly-wise, the weight of tradition seemed to be making itself felt. I was the man. In the final analysis, it was up to me to protect her and provide for her. As I say, there was nothing at all logical about this feeling — and I had never felt this way about Hilary. Hilary and I, of course, had never lived together and possibly it would have been different if we had, but while we were together it was always on a footing of jointness, but non-dependence — like a binary sun, two equal orbs revolving round each other at the centre of their own system. This may have been inaccurate in astronomical terms, but it was my image of what a modern relationship ought to be. And, indeed, it was still basically my sense of how things would be between Bea and me. Nevertheless, and in spite of myself, I could not rid myself of the feeling that it was now my job to look after her, and compelled, as always, to assign this feeling some significance, I took it that it was probably a sign of increasing maturity, both in myself and in the relationship.

When we got back to the flat, we dumped all Bea's stuff into the spare room, had a bite to eat, then went to bed and made love as if it was the last day of the world.

From the next morning, Bea started to change my life.

10

That statement is true, but it is leaping ahead slightly. I came home from work the first evening, hoping against hope that she would still be there. I recalled how, on the evening of the first day after she had irrupted back into my life, I had rather hoped she would be gone when I got back. I felt, superstitiously, that poetic justice might turn the tables on me: she stayed then, when I didn't want her; she would be gone now, when I did. In fact, for many days after that I would come home in trepidation that she had been merely taking a holiday from her parents or her old life and would vanish back to one or the other — or, that she would reach clarity about what she really wanted to do with her future and go off and do it.

That first morning I had left not really having much idea what she would do with the day — perhaps unpack her things, perhaps start thinking about a job and maybe even looking for one, perhaps just chill out and get used to being in London again. It didn't really matter what she did, she could have spent the whole day in bed if she had wanted to, just so long as she was still there. She was, although I panicked momentarily and internally when I found the living room empty and was relieved more than titillated when I heard her voice sing out 'Come and join me' from the bathtub.

After an agreeable wallow, we returned to the living room — she in her dressing gown again and with a pyramid of towel on her head. She sat down on the sofa and picked up a notepad and pencil from the coffee table.

'Don't think I've been sitting around all day, waiting for you to come home,' she said, giving me a kiss. 'I've been feeling domestic. Look at this.'

'What's this?'

'It's a plan. First, answer me one question truly, honestly, so help you God etc. Do you like this flat the way it is?'

'I suppose so. Don't you?'

'Am I in your good books?'

'Of course you're in my good books.'

'Promise you won't stop loving me if I say your flat is grotty?'

'It could do with a lick of paint here and there — and I still love you.'

'Nigel, as long as you're insured, it could do with a visit from your friendly neighbourhood arsonist. Or …'

'Or what?'

'Or you can let me do it over for you. I know it's my first day … no, it's not my first day, I've been here before and you slept chastely on this very sofa … I know it's a liberty, but I feel full of energy and I know I could make it really nice for you.'

'For us.'

'For us. Thank you. Now …'

And she outlined her plans for attacking the various rooms in turn, suggested what she'd like to do with them, and produced a sheaf of colour charts that she'd got from the local DIY store.

'Have you done this before?' I asked.

'No. But I know I can do it, I've got a magazine — tra la!' she flourished it 'and a manual. If I start in the second bedroom, I can get my hand in before I tackle anywhere important. Is it a deal?'

'What's my side of the deal?'

'You can do the cooking and make love to me every night except Thursdays.'

'Why not Thursdays?'

'All right, Thursdays too, but then I get to throw out some of this old stuff that's cluttering up the lounge. Nigel Anderson, you need a woman in your life. I am that woman.

Go and cook me something before I starve and you go back to being a sad, sexless bachelor.'

Consequently, for the next several weeks, I would come home, getting less apprehensive as the days went by, to find Bea, in a pair of spattered dungarees with her hair in a knot on top of her head and the old cap on that was a relic of her countryside 'blending-in' gear, perched on top of a stepladder or smothered in wallpaper or working away on a portable workbench she had acquired.

There were a few disasters — like the first time she tried to hang wallpaper and when she overreached herself in the plumbing department — but, by and large, the transformation she wrought on the flat — I wouldn't say 'my flat' and still thought it was tempting providence to say 'our flat', so it was 'the flat' — was a tremendous success. My role was not confined to fulfilling the conditions of the original deal. I helped out at the weekends and wrote cheques — not all the cheques, because Bea was in 'money no object' mode as far as her personal finances were concerned and contributed generously. In addition, I had to inspect and approve everything solemnly, and help her plan the next day's agenda.

She seemed very happy. She said it was very peaceful working away on her own at her own pace. It was enormously satisfying to take a bare wall or a bare ceiling and cover it with lining paper and then cover the paper with paint. It was wonderful to be doing something useful for a change. She said that in her houses in America … 'Wasn't this all a terrible comedown?' I interjected. No it wasn't, because they were palaces, they were perfect, they had been decorated by Mrs Guildersleeve Senior, or the first Mrs Guildersleeve Junior, or an interior designer from Madison Avenue, in the most impeccable taste, and it was absolutely forbidden to change or rearrange anything. Not that there might not come a time to sell this flat and move to somewhere … well, possibly a little bigger. But, basically, this was the real thing, and if you were going to change your life, it was sensible to start from the bottom up with your living accommodation; getting a social life, getting a job, could wait a little while.

When only the kitchen was left to be given the treatment, Bea proposed that it was time to think about a flat-rewarming party. Phase two of the master plan — revive our social life — was to begin.

The original list of invitees seemed pretty pathetic. It consisted of my boss and her husband, the couple who had invited me over to be paired off with Jill, the secretary/admin person at work and her partner, the gay couple in the next-door flat, a chap I had known at university and occasionally met up with for a drink and his girlfriend whom I'd never met, and ... and after that it was scraping-the-barrel time. After Bea had commented on the sadness of my contribution, she added her own, which was, if anything, even sadder. A former boyfriend — how former? — very former ... if he was still living at the same address. Two friends of her father's plus wives and, if we were really desperate to fill floor space, a friend of her mother's. Average age of potential ravers — forty-five plus.

'This is ridiculous,' she said. 'There are six or seven million people in this city, why don't we know any of them?'

'It just isn't easy to met people in London. How did you meet people in New York?'

'I just did.'

'Shall we drop the idea?'

'No way, we need to get to know people. All right, be very sociable at work. Invite everyone who's not actually a recluse or a psychopath, and let's see what happens.'

The party — in a gleaming flat, decorated in colours inspired by a Paul Klee painting which was a particular favourite of Bea's and with numerous other, as they seemed to me, highly imaginative touches — was a brilliant success.

When Bea set out to be charming, she could charm the birds from the trees. Moving among the guests and keeping the drink flowing, I could feel my stock rising simply through being the man who had brought this witty and accomplished woman within everyone's ken. The ex-boyfriend did come, but with his wife. The woman who had introduced me to Jill apologized for having thought I was in need of her matchmaking skills (such as they were) and made me give an account of how Bea and I had got together — something it was quite difficult to do in a few sentences in a party-apposite manner and without giving too much away. Finally, one of Bea's father's friends, having been told by Bea that I was the mind behind the forthcoming Great Business Minds series, pinned me into a corner and lectured me at considerable length about the dearth of serious management literature in the UK as compared to the US, ignoring my admittedly throwaway protests that I was not the originator of the project and my real interest was fiction, and finished by asking if I would mind if he mentioned my name to a friend of his — who just happened to be the chairman of a publishing company twice the size of the one I was currently working for.

By the time the last guests had gone and we collapsed amid the rubble, it seemed that another milestone had been successfully passed — we had appeared in public together, as the society pages might have said. We had achieved something as a couple. We had allowed ourselves to be inspected and sanctioned as a couple by a rather disparate group of people, thanks to whom we could, with luck, expect our social horizons to expand over time. Things were definitely looking up.

11

In one respect, however, we were still something of an anomaly. We were not a working couple. There are certain slots that individuals and couples are supposed to fit into. We had presented ourselves at the party as a newly established but stable partnership in the early stages of upward mobility. And that was true enough. Yet in one sense, I was in the position of a man who keeps a wife or mistress simply to look after his home and entertain for him — an absurd position for someone with my modest income and equally modest domestic and social circumstances. The fact that Bea was contributing to our living and upward mobility expenses out of her divorce settlement was something I wasn't particularly keen to advertise. Nor, I think, was she. One or two people at the party had asked me what Bea did. I said 'she's looking for something suitable'. The last thing I wanted to do was to suggest that there was anything temporary about our relationship and that Bea was living with me while she decided what shape her future might take, as if there might not be a role for me in that future. We needed to define ourselves more precisely as a social entity. More importantly, we needed, for our own sakes, to have a clearer sense of where we were going, now that we had found each other and proved to ourselves, as I hoped we had, that we could live together successfully. Most importantly of all — and I was particularly mindful of Bea's father's advice that she should not be allowed to get bored — now that she had refurbished the flat and launched us on a social life, Bea needed a role, a function, basically, a job.

Some time during the week after the party I decided that it was perhaps time to try to grasp this nettle. When I came home in the evening, I asked her what she'd been doing that day. She held up a copy of *Dombey and Son* that she was half way through.

'You don't get bored?'

'Reading Dickens?'

'I meant sitting in the flat all day.'

'Nigel, I worked my ass off to get this place into shape. Aren't I entitled to sit and enjoy it a little?'

'Of course you are. Did anything happen?'

'There was a murder on the staircase and I got a strippergram from Prince Charles. What happened to you?'

'It was just an ordinary day.'

'Well, it was just an ordinary day here too. I like ordinary days. Give me a kiss.'

I kissed her.

'Now shut up and let me finish this chapter and then you can teach me how to cook spaghetti.'

This became something of a pattern. Her days seemed to vary very little. She finished *Dombey* and began *Our Mutual Friend*; she finished *Our Mutual Friend* and began *Little Dorrit*. She had worked her ass off etc, and now she was not just relaxing, she was feeding her mind. Did I realize how little chance she had had just to read since she left university? No, I didn't, and as long as she was happy, I didn't mind — I was envious, in fact, because, apart from anything else, it made me realize how much time I had to spend reading stuff from work that was far less entertaining and stimulating.

Never quite free from anxiety — what would happen when she got to *Edwin Drood*? — I was nonetheless very happy, and there wasn't really a problem with money, so why worry?. And she didn't spend all her time reading. She got a friendship going with Mary, the woman who had introduced me to Jill, and started having coffee with her once or twice a week. Mary had two small children and worked part-time from home. Through Mary, Bea met other women — other mothers with children at the same school and kindergarten as Mary's mainly. If I had thought that Bea was not interested in friendships with other women, I was obviously wrong — or she had changed. Mary and her husband Jimmy, my colleague, invited us for dinner, and we had them back, together with another couple from the little network that Bea had entered. The social side of things was developing nicely, even the family side of things developed. We had little contact with Bea's parents, though postcards arrived occasionally from the Far East or Africa when her father was on business trips, but answering the phone once when my mother rang and I was out for some reason, Bea had got into a long and apparently very friendly conversation with her. Further calls during the daytime followed, with the same message being relayed to me every time and repeated in conversations I had with my mother myself ... when was I bringing Bea to meet the family; why hadn't we come ages ago; was I, my mother at last enquired indignantly, ashamed of them?

There was no answer to that, and a visit was arranged. The fact was that in a way I was ashamed. I was madly in love with Bea. I did not hold an exactly exalted view of her, but I thought her extraordinary, exotic, not the sort of 'girl' one took home to meet one's Mum and Dad. There was the class thing — her folks were much better off and grander than my folks, even if they behaved abominably and were in a state of constant warfare with each other. There were all sorts of things that all added up to the sense that I had somehow acquired Bea under false pretences, and taking her back to my origins was a surefire way of revealing the imposture. The romance would cease, and I should be left desolate again.

With this pathetic lack of self-confidence, I seem to have spent an awful lot of my life preparing myself to bite bullets. And lo, on this occasion as on many others, the bullet was as soft as butter. Bea wasn't a snob — at least not a social snob. She submitted to my mother's ministrations gracefully, deployed all her charm, and — while my mother took me out to the kitchen first to castigate me for keeping this paragon under wraps for so long, then to congratulate me for finding someone who was even sweeter than Hilary, and lastly, taking my head in both her hands and speaking to me in an urgent whisper, to say 'don't lose her, please don't lose her' — Bea finally managed to extract a promise from my father that he would go and see the doctor.

That was the only cloud over that weekend. It must have been a long time since I had seen him, because my father seemed to me to be shockingly changed — much greyer and thinner than I remembered. Only incredible obstinacy or prophetic fear could have been keeping him from going to seek medical help. My mother and I came back into the living room to find Bea sitting on the sofa holding his hand between both of hers and refusing to let go or stop imploring him with all her body and eye language until he gave in. This was something my mother never forgot. And, when we had all relaxed a bit, and my mother had regaled Bea with the dreaded account of my origins, Bea regaled them back with a few reminiscences of me as a student and a brief account of her own career along the lines of 'I was wild and reckless in my youth and made a lot of mistakes, but I've grown up now and, thank God, I found your wonderful son again and what an incredible difference he has made to my life I can't tell you.' After that, however her parents might feel, there were two elders for whom Bea could do no wrong, and, as far I was I was concerned, if she chose to spend the rest of her life reading her way through the classics and drinking coffee, then it was all right with me.

My father kept his promise and went to see the doctor and was sent to hospital for tests and, as my mother had feared and as he had probably feared even more, was told he had cancer. But he was also told that the cancer was probably operable. He was taken into hospital almost immediately and operated on. The surgeon announced that the operation had been successful: the cancer had been removed. There was a chance that the cancer would return, but he was hopeful, 'very hopeful', my mother said, that it would not.

These developments naturally kept the whole family in a state of terrible suspense for several weeks. Dave came down from Lincolnshire to stay with my mother while my father was in hospital, I came up from London as often as I could, and either I or Bea rang every day. The surgeon's announcement was greeted with extraordinary relief, and when my father had come home and convalesced for a month or two, he did seem much better and was able to resume his usual routine.

In the meantime, however, there had been, for me, an even more momentous announcement. Bea told me she was pregnant.

12

Since this was a fairly natural consequence of banging away enthusiastically several times a week, I ought not to have been surprised, I suppose, but I was. I had assumed … well, as far as I recall, mindful of the efficient Jill and of Bea's dreadful memories of New York, I had at some point in the very early stages of our being together come home with a packet of condoms and offered to put one on, and Bea's response had been a pained look or a protesting 'please!' or possibly a 'That won't be necessary'. In any case, I was by no means reluctant to dispense with rubbers and rigmarole in favour of free, unfettered bonking on demand, and there was too much going on — and it was all too delightful — to give the matter any further thought. Nor did we ever afterwards discuss the how and why, and whether the pregnancy was accident or design or helped on its way by baby-clubbing in Mary's circle, because there was so much else to think about and look forward to. It was a happy coincidence that Bea had painted the walls of the spare bedroom sky blue and the ceiling in a pinkish shade of white — and the key word in that sentence and, indeed, ultimately in the whole experience was 'happy'.

I came home on the fateful evening to find her stretched out on the sofa with a book in the normal way. I kissed her in passing on the way to the bathroom and bedroom to get out of my office clothes, keeping up the usual small-talk commentary on what had happened in the course of the day, came back, lifted her feet up off the end of the sofa, sat down, cradling her feet on my lap, and asked her what sort of day she'd had and how she was getting on with *Wives and Daughters*, for she had by now sufficiently replenished her mind with Dickens and George Eliot and was getting to grips with the rest of the mid-Victorian period. Her response was to fold down the top corner of the page, close the book, and place it on the coffee table so that I could read the title — *Natural Childbirth*. She looked at me meaningfully.

'What are you reading that for? ... ... Oh!'

'Oh my God or ...?'

'Are you?'

'I tested myself; I think so. I'm going to see the doctor in the morning.'

'Oh my God!'

I sat there gaping, trying to take it in.

'How ...?'

'Nigel, use your imagination. I'll get you a drink.'

'No. I meant ... How do you feel?'

'I feel fine.'

'I mean about the baby.'

'I meant about the baby. Nigel, I want it. I'm happy. Are you?'

'Yes, well — no, yes. If you ...'

'It's our baby, it's not just mine. I will keep it. I just hope to God, it's really there and I can.'

'You sit tight, I'll get myself ...'

'No ...' She hitched herself up so that she was sitting cross-legged at one end of the sofa and took both my hands in hers. 'Say that you're pleased. Please?'

'I am pleased. I'm just trying to get my head round it.'

'I can do this on my own. I don't want to do it on my own, but ...'

'For God's sake, Bea, I love you. I wouldn't ...'

'Some men would.'

'I'm not "some men". The worst thing I can imagine is losing you. I didn't think ... I wasn't sure you wanted children.'

'Well, one at a time ...'

'You know what I mean. I am pleased.'

'Because I didn't want to give Rich his bloody son and heir doesn't mean ...'

'Bugger Richard! If it's what *you* want ...'

'Don't go on about it's being what I want as if I'm being dictated to by my biological clock or something. If you wanted to wait till I was forty, or till we'd moved into a bigger place, or till we were married ...'

'I'm not saying it's bad time, I'm just stupefied. Pinch me and say it again.'

She leant forward and pinched both my cheeks: 'You stupefied son of a bitch, I'm having a baby! Don't pinch me. Just say you're pleased.'

'I'm pleased.'

She took my hand and placed it on her breast. 'You'll have to share this with someone else.'

'As long as it's just the baby.'

'Get off!' She pretended to push my hand away, then said 'Show me you're pleased. Take me to bed.'

* * *

The more I thought about it, the more pleased I got. Bea wouldn't allow any champagne celebrations or anyone to be told, until she'd received confirmation from her GP. By then, if the news had been that it was a false alarm, it would have been a bitter disappointment to us both. The news was good, however, and it was rapturously received by my mother, received with warm congratulations by our friends, and went down at Hell Hall like the proverbial lead balloon or, more accurately perhaps, like the *Hindenburg*.

I got Bea's end of the telephone conversation.

'Mother, it's me.'

... ...

'Yes, I'm sorry I haven't rung ...'

... ...

'Well, you didn't ring me either, and I *am* still living with him. Listen, do you want to hear my news or not? Is Dad there?'

...

'Well, do you have a number for him in Hong Kong?'

… … … …

'I'm not just using you as directory enquiries. If you'll shut up a minute, I'll tell you what it's about. (Oh God!)' This last was an aside to me with her hand over the mouthpiece.

… … …

'Yes, I'm sorry. All right, brace yourself. I'm pregnant.'

'Mother, hello? Are you there?'

… …

'I'm pregnant, mother, I'm having a baby! And yes, I am sure, and yes, I've seen the doctor …'

… … …

'Yes, it bloody well is his!'

… … … … … … … … … … … … … … … … … …
… … … … … … … … … … … … … …

'You fucking well talk to her!' And she handed me the receiver and started pacing up and down the room in a rage.

'… of all the stupid, stupid tricks to play! You haven't the first idea what you're letting yourself in for, you haven't the first idea what it takes to be a mother, and as for the penniless publisher, if he thinks that by getting you in the club he's setting himself up with a nice little country place in Wiltshire, then he can think again. Even your father agrees with me on that. Four years you were with Richard, four years! And don't think your father will say any different, because he'd be just as delighted to be that useless bastard's bastard's grandfather as I would. How could you, Beatrice, how could you? … Beatrice?'

'It's the penniless publisher.'

'Put my daughter back on the line.'

I held the receiver out to Bea. 'Tell her to fuck off!'

'She doesn't want to talk to you.'

There was a snort of exasperation. 'Tell her I'm sending her the address of a man in Harley Street. I'll pay. Tell her if she's got a grain of sense left, she'll see him and sort her life out while she's got the chance.'

'I'm sorry, I misled you a moment ago. What she actually said was "tell her to fuck off" — that's from both of us.'

And I put the phone down, trembling with fury.

'What did I do to have such a bitch for a mother?' cried Bea, and burst into tears.

'It's all right,' I said, taking her in my arms. 'It'll be all right.'

'I don't want to talk to her again. I don't want to talk to her. She'll make me lose the baby.'

'She won't, she won't, calm down.'

'God, if you *ever* see *any* sign that I'm getting like her, throttle me. I couldn't bear it. Oh this poor baby!'

'It'll be fine.'

'It won't be fine if it keeps getting doused in fury juice and adrenalin. You've got to keep her away from me, Nigel. You've got to keep her away from me.'

'I will, I will.'

Gradually, she quietened, only to tense up again shortly afterwards, when the phone rang.

'I'll get it,' I said, though I hesitated slightly before picking up. 'Hello?'

'Hello — er ... Nigel.'

('It's your father!') Bea half got up to come to the phone, then stopped and gave me a look which I interpreted as a request to check for flak before handing over to her.

'Hello, how are you?'

'Can I speak to Bea?'

'She's just ... Can I help?'

'I'm calling from Hong Kong. Just put her on, please.'

'She's just been talking to her mother. She's a bit upset.'

'Her mother's incandescent. She's just chewed my ear off.'

'I meant Bea's upset. If *you* feel like chewing anyone's ear off, would you mind saving it for another time?'

'Look, this call is clocking up hundreds of dollars, let me speak to her.'

'I don't want her upset.'

'I'm not going to upset her. I think you're a bloody fool … still, I suppose it takes two to tango. Are you going to stick with her?'

'Yes.'

'Is she all right about it?'

'Yes.'

'Right, fine. Now, please, let me speak to her.'

('I think it's OK') I handed her the phone. 'Dad?' she said and burst into tears again.

* * *

Her father was reasonably OK about it. At least Bea was able to talk to him sensibly and reassure him that she was happy about the whole thing and that it was not some dastardly plot on my part to bind her to me for ever and take over the family silver and businesses and lord it in Hell Hall after his ashes had been scattered by shotgun over his favourite rabbit warren in the Vale of Pewsey.

The process of defining ourselves socially as a couple, of course, took a step forward, though it became questionable whether we would be able to sustain any upward momentum when there were three of us and still only one income to support the family — especially since we were both determined, at first privately and separately, and then openly and together, that there would be more than one. This little one, if, please God, it made its way safely into the world, was not going to be an only child.

I never knew precisely how much Bea's divorce settlement from Richard amounted to. I knew it was pretty large, by my standards, and that her father had helped her invest some of it. Whenever I mentioned it, Bea simply said that everything was fine and there was nothing to worry about. But I received a financial boost irrespective of any contribution from Bea when the old boy network came good and the friend of the friend of Bea's father offered me a job at a salary roughly a third as much again as I had been earning previously. The down side was that I was being hired to oversee an encyclopaedia of management — but that was a minor matter. I said goodbye to the offices in Golden Square and moved to newer and larger premises in Holborn. On this basis, it did not seem unreasonable to plan a move to larger domestic premises as well. House prices were rocketing upwards, but so was the value of the flat. We worked out that if I put in the equity from the flat, Bea put in an equal sum, and we doubled the present mortgage, we would be able to afford a house of the type most of our friends were living in — namely a largish, three-bedroomed, Victorian terrace in a decent area, hopefully with some interesting features and a small garden.

As Bea's belly began to swell gently, our hopes and expectations swelled mightily. 'What-forism' was entirely a thing of the past. I had a purpose, and my eyes were bright with it. The premonition of responsibility I had had on the train back from Wiltshire was obviously a timely one, but responsibility was not a burden. It was a spur, a touchstone of a man's mettle. I would prove equal to the challenge. I would earn plenty of bloody money, put bread on the bloody table, and bloody well get on. Basta!

There was, of course, the small question of whether the child whose first kicks and judders were now starting to make themselves felt and who was now a hazily visible entity on the ultrasound screen (we asked not to be told the sex), was going to come into the world in or out of wedlock.

13

My opinion of marriage has since altered more in tone than in substance, which is to say that it seemed to me then and now to be mainly a question of a piece of official paper, legal status, certain financial advantages and commitments, and not much else. Perhaps I had felt differently long before when I had gone down on one knee in the dust in France and proposed to Hilary, I cannot remember. At the time about which I am writing, I lived with no other thought than to love and be loved by Bea. Feeling, I believed, was everything; all the rest was a formality. I did not, frankly, care deep down whether we got married or not, so long as she loved me and everything was all right. Not that I was actively averse to marriage, especially marriage to Bea. I was ready to marry her on the spot if, by that means, I could make our relationship more secure. But it was patently obvious that marriage did not necessarily bind two people together with hoops of steel. Among my new colleagues was one who was going through a messy divorce. Not only that but she was getting divorced after a mere eighteen months of marriage. Not only that but the eighteen disastrous months of marriage had followed upon six perfectly happy years of living in sin. 'If it ain't broke, don't fix it' was her word to people in my position.

Almost more of a deterrent than Alice — she of the six fat years and the eighteen lean months — was Roger, who was planning to marry his fiancée in eighteen months time (the concurrence of the two time spans was purely fortuitous) and when I say planning, I mean, putting approximately as much effort into preparing for the big day as NASA put into the average space shot.

When I first met Roger, I got the impression that he and his beloved (Samantha, a market researcher) spent all their leisure time scouring London and the Home Counties for a suitable church (with at least eight bells) to hold the ceremony in, preferably not too far from a suitably classy, but not too hideously expensive (everything was minutely budgeted) venue for the reception. And when they weren't examining AA Guides and interrogating vicars — because they envisaged several additions and alterations to the standard liturgical form ('for richer and richer, for better and better — this is meant to be a joyful occasion for God's sake!') and unearthing organists who could play the final movement of Beethoven's *Ninth*, they were leafing through travel brochures. It was Bali (for the honeymoon, that is), then it was Peru, then it was Australia, then it was Bali again. For this was to be the day of days, the event of events, the pinnacle of their lives to date (and Samantha's best friend had been taken to church by four white horses, entertained her guests on a steamer on the Thames, and had her first married fuck — well, actually in the toilet of a 747, but officially at a beach hotel in the Bahamas). When I innocently asked Roger whether eighteen months ahead wasn't perhaps a bit early, he looked at me pityingly as if I had dropped in off the planet Ignorance and explained that they were actually leaving it rather late, and so great was the rush to altars and register offices in the months of decent weather that everything had to be nailed down years in advance. 'It's not bloody beer and sandwiches in the living room and a weekend in Brighton, is it? Christ, this is a proper wedding!'

With virginity in short supply and everyone apparently enjoying seamless, socially sanctioned sex from their mid teens, this is the new *droit de seigneur*: everyone's right to lord it for one day in fancy dress in front of their friends and relatives, and for a fortnight or more on a lounger by the pool, on the beach, on safari, watching the sun go down over film-set scenery, storing up video footage for the amusement and envy of everyone back home, treated like nobs and nabobs by smilingly complaisant denizens of the Third World. And why not? If you can get it, take it. Show them you know how to live. It would seem like sour grapes on the part of someone who actually had a two-day honeymoon in Brighton to criticize the Balinese brigade.

Is there necessarily more spiritual worth in discovering the joys and awkwardnesses of sex in a boarding house in Blackpool than in achieving well-practised orgasms in a four-poster elegantly draped in mosquito netting in a swish hotel somewhere east of Suez? Who knows? I have realized that it is easy to confuse a grudging, puritanical mindset with spiritual superiority. It is equally easy to spot spiritual shallowness, because it is everywhere and for all time. If to spend an hour contemplating a Rembrandt or listening to a Bruckner symphony, or to stand perfectly alone and still in the midst of some breathtaking scenery or to see the stars in the night sky so multitudinous and bright that it feels as if you could reach up and collect them in your hand, or to have a sparrow alight on your shoulder or to feel a baby's fingers curl around your finger, means more to you than any number of package tours with free piña coladas ... then lucky you, I think. No, I actually believe that. But does that mean piña colada drinkers are incapable of insight or feeling? No, it doesn't.

The truth is that Roger and Samantha's lavish wedding ushered in a marriage that lasted longer than ours. Nevertheless, I thought he was a boring sod with as much sense of the true realities of human life as the weekend magazine in the average quality newspaper.

Whatever my views on weddings, the idea of asking Bea to marry me was exercising my mind and, since there was positive pressure in that direction coming from my family and negative pressure (though with positive effect) coming from hers, it worried me that, if what Roger and Samantha were planning constituted a 'proper wedding' and was what the average woman expected, then how on earth was I going to organize anything of the kind in the time available, let alone find the money to pay for it?

The obvious solution was to talk to Bea about it. But it did not seem right to approach the woman I loved with a cheery 'What do you think about us getting married? I'm in two minds about it myself'. On the other hand, if there was something on Bea's mind, she didn't waste time shilly-shallying, she either came straight out with it or at least took care to craft an opportunity for discussion to take place. In this instance, when she was about five months gone, after I had been with her to the hospital for a scan and we were making our way home in a taxi, she turned to me and asked: 'Are you worried that this little thing is going to be born a bastard?'

'It's not my biggest worry, no. So long as it's born all right and you're all right …'

'That's what you always say. Everything's got to be all right with you, just all right. We're all right, oh wonderful! That's all right. Can't you imagine anything better than all right?'

'Does it worry you then?'

'No.' She stared moodily out of the taxi window.

'Look, we haven't actually discussed this …'

'What's to discuss?'

'I haven't exactly heard you singing the praises of marriage.'

'You bastard!' She exclaimed, then knocked on the glass panel. 'Stop the taxi!'

'Bea!'

'Stop, here!'

The taxi screeched to a halt. She got out and slammed the door shut before I could stop her.

'Can you wait here?' I asked the driver.

'No, mate, double yellow.'

'God! Keep going slowly.' Bea was striding out down the road.

'I'll do my best, mate. Got to watch the traffic. They get bloody funny, when they're in the family way. What do you want me to do, crawl along beside her?'

'If you can.'

'When my girlfriend was expecting our last one ...'

'Yes, hang on.' I wound the window down. 'Bea, get in the taxi, please.'

'Bugger off!'

'Bea, please!' The taxi had to stop at a red light. Bea strode on across the junction. Heads turned in our direction.

'There's only two ways of arguing with a woman, mate, and they're both wrong. What's it all about anyway?'

'Getting married, I suppose. Bea!!'

'Mug's game, that is. Anyway, she only bloody shut me out of the bedroom ...'

'Sorry, who?'

'My girlfriend. Wouldn't let me touch her. Well, two can play at that game. I went and stayed at my mother's, took the kid with me and all.' The lights changed. He put the taxi into gear and moved off again. 'Went out for a good time ... you know. Made sure some of her friends saw me ...'

'Yes. Bea!'

No response.

'All right. Bea, will you marry me?'

She stopped. The taxi stopped — and reversed fractionally so that the rear door was right beside her. Other heads turned.

'No!' said Bea and walked on again.

'I think you're wasting your time there, mate. But I'll tell you what. I'll drive on — like, sod you then, you know. Then we'll pull in round the next corner. Trust me, when she gets there, she'll get in.' And he pulled out and accelerated away.

'Wait!'

'Trust me. A week later she was round at my mother's ever so bloody humble. You can't let them walk all over you, know what I mean?' He took the next turning on the left and stopped.

'I hope you're right.'

'I know London and I know women. I had a bloke in here once ...' I forget what the bloke did. I looked out of rear window waiting for Bea to appear at the street corner. She didn't. I got out of the taxi, against the driver's advice, and stood by the door. She still didn't appear. I went to the corner and looked back down the main road. Shit! No sign of her. I went back and paid off the taxi ... 'Never mind, mate, could be a lucky escape' ... then went back down the main road looking for her. After half an hour frantically running in and out of shops and cafés and checking the bus queues, I gave up and tried to flag down another taxi to take me home, assuming, correctly, that she must have rumbled the taximan's little ploy and made her own way back. When no taxis responded, I finally got the bus.

She was sitting on the sofa in slightly bulky elegance reading Trollope again and eating a bar of chocolate. 'You were saying?' she said.

14

In the end it was a sort of lesson in how to get married with anti-style. There are arrangements to be made and things to be organized ahead of even the least pretentious of weddings, so Bea went to book a slot at the register office on what she calculated roughly would be the ninth day of the ninth month of her pregnancy, a Saturday in early August 1986 — and got one thanks to a cancellation. It was to be a huge occasion, as she said.

There was no question of asking the Major to shell out for anything (though he did send a decent cheque), indeed, since relations with Hell Hall had been non-existent since the fatal phone call and the ceremonial tearing-up of the letter with the address of the Harley Street abortionist to the quality. There was some doubt as to whether Bea's mother would actually turn up to throw a little vitriol as we came out. In the event she did come, joining a guest list, which, apart from the furthest reaches of family on both sides, comprised mainly our London friends. After some hesitation, I wrote to RT and Caroline at the last address I had for them, but received no reply.

There was no question either of sending the invitees off to Harrods or John Lewis's to consult an official present list. When suggestions that 'something imaginative would be nice' were met with the derision they deserved, Bea typed out a list on a little Amstrad word-processor she had bought herself and set up in the soon-to-be nursery and distributed it to all and sundry. The upshot still was that we began married life with enough tablecloths to stock a small hotel and not a great deal else.

My mother's imaginary daughter would doubtless have got married in white in the village church. Mother had been to a punk and socialist wedding … after the register office formalities Dave and Maisie had their 'proper wedding' at the working men's club, walked in to 'The Red Flag', promised to share the crap and the cream and to be good to each other and the earth and all its creatures, and signalled the end of the solemnities with 'I am an Anarchist' ... now she was set to attend another which bore all the hallmarks of a shotgun wedding, apart from the presence of the shotgun, and with the Major in attendance there was perhaps no guarantee even of that. But she bore it all with remarkable composure and was liberal in her offers of help, though my father's health was giving her, giving us all, cause for concern again.

Came the great day and the bride — 'there's only going to be one marquee at this wedding' — clad in volumes of light blue floating stuff to match the colour of her eyes, with a plunging décolletage, her lovely long blonde hair brushed out over her shoulders, a broad-brimmed straw hat on, and carrying a small bouquet of violets, travelled to the town hall, at her own insistence, alone and by taxi, to ensure that her arrival could not be taken absolutely for granted. She nevertheless arrived, to be met by her father in his army uniform and her two 'supporters', also equipped as minimal paramedics in case of emergency, Mary and her other friend, Daisy, in matching cream outfits with pencil skirts and waist-hugging tops. At the top of the steps waited myself in a new suit with a dark red waistcoat, Dave as best man, in a suit borrowed from our father, and the rest of the throng. We waddled up the aisle, made our vows, kissed passionately, and waddled back down again. My mother cried, Bea's mother grimaced, our friends threw confetti in defiance of the bylaws, and the two supporters produced matching blue-and-cream football rattles from inside their matching bags and produced an unholy din. Some photographs were taken. Everyone clambered into a fleet of waiting taxis and we set off for a nearby pub with a large upper room, where speeches were made ('There were some who told me I couldn't *give* my daughter away ...' 'Those of us who have known Nigel for a long time must be pleasantly surprised to find that he does obviously know one end of a woman from the other after all ...'), champagne was drunk, liberal quantities of bangers and mash were consumed, dances were danced — that is, Bea and I clasped each other like sumo wrestlers around the bump and kissed and twirled gently until she started to feel giddy — the only momentary hiatus in the merriment — then we got into another taxi to Victoria station, clattering cans behind us in the good old-fashioned way, and rode first-class to Brighton. I managed to carry her to the threshold in the hotel — the door wasn't wide enough to carry her through it — and we collapsed on the bed and laughed and kissed ourselves to sleep thinking it had, when all was said and done, been a bloody good day.

It was a good day; it was a happy day, enjoyed by everyone except probably Bea's parents. And the next two days, very gentle slow-moving days necessarily, were good too. We thought it unwise to stay away longer than two days in case the little one took it into its head to make an entrance before its cue. But the fact that Bea consented to style herself Mrs Anderson did not make me love her any more than I did all ready, and the fact that our friends had witnessed an exchange of rings and vows did not knit us together more securely than we were already knit. It was not the tying of the knot that made the difference, but the cutting of the cord. The baby was born on the 31st of August, a little girl to be known as Anne or Annie. Then, as I held Bea, who was propped up in the hospital bed holding the baby while the midwife still fussed around her other end, and we were both absolutely centred on this yawning red scrap, wrapped in a towel, with a crest of dark hair, then I felt surely we two are one, we three are one, we cannot get closer, it cannot be better than this.

Part 2

Breaking

15

After our marriage and Annie's birth, I was as confident as I could be that our relationship was a good and true one, and that it would last. Since that confidence proved to be wholly and miserably mistaken, I have spent many bitter hours trying to work out why everything fell apart. Let's look on the bright side, however. We had six or seven good years before the three or four bad months (that was all it took, in effect) that killed us off. 'They can't take those away from me', as the song says — though they, whoever they are, can have a bloody good try. In fact, you can do the job for yourself easily enough with recriminations and self-pity. Nothing looks quite the same from the perspective of failure and regret; you have to fight the inclination to see events that were simple occasions for happiness, sadness, encouragement, or frustration as symptoms of inevitable disaster.

We took Annie home to the flat and, like all new parents, experienced the enormous, life-changing upheaval that comes with having a baby about the place. There were no more hours in the day to cope with all the additional routine procedures needed to keep her fed, clean, and comforted, and there seemed to be far fewer hours in the night. We had her in a Moses basket inside a cot placed by Bea's side of the bed, so that, in theory at least, when she cried in the night Bea could simply lean over, pick her up, and plug her in to the nipple, without necessarily fully waking up herself or disturbing me. But Bea soon found that she was waking up in advance of the baby crying and when she woke up and sat up, I tended to wake up too. We longed, as everyone does, for the baby to get older and start to sleep through. At the same time, as I think everyone else also does too, we found it hard to bear the thought that each delightful stage or manifestation of babyhood had inevitably to pass and be succeeded by the next. That was the overarching impression of that time: all inconveniences — the broken nights, the dirty nappies, the panics when the baby did anything the least out of the ordinary — all those aside, it was a delight. We were enraptured. Bea looked blooming and fulfilled. I might stagger off to work and yawn with more than usual intensity over the business of getting the Business Encyclopaedia together, but I came home with an even greater sense that this was where I lived, moved, and had my being.

About six months after the birth, when Annie was starting to be weaned, we put the plan to move house into operation. We had no trouble finding a buyer for the flat or in finding a house that we liked, though at a slightly higher price than we had originally envisaged — we were gazumped, but by then Bea had set her heart on the place, and anyway it seemed that the upward revaluation of bricks and mortar was an unstoppable process — the flat had virtually doubled in value in the time I had occupied it — so we went ahead without too many worries, moving in just in time for Annie's first birthday.

We were now in Hornsey, just down the road really from where we were before. People told us the schools in the area were quite good, but we weren't really thinking ahead that far. Bea's settlement was getting somewhat depleted, but I was earning well. The house was even in reasonable decorative order, so we just dumped ourselves and our stuff in it and took our time about getting it sorted out. In fact we made no attempt to redecorate it thoroughly until Bea fell pregnant again, which prompted another round of nest-building or rather nest-refurbishment, which, in turn, such seems to be the way of things, was the prelude to another removal. But that is jumping ahead.

We were sufficiently up together by that first Christmas in Hornsey to invite my parents over for Christmas Day. This fact is worth noting because it was the only time my father visited the house. Towards the end of January, he had to go back into hospital again for tests and another operation. I went with my mother on the afternoon after the operation. When we asked for news, we were immediately taken aside and ushered into a small room by a senior nursing sister. She looked grave.

'The news is not good, I'm afraid, Mrs Anderson.'

'Is he …?

'He has about a month.'

'Oh no, oh but surely …'

'The cancer's spread. Mr Smith has done what he could, but it's spread too far, you see. There's nothing more we can do. We've done what we can to make him comfortable. I'm sorry, I know this must come as a shock.'

'Yes.'

'Can we speak to Mr Smith?' I asked, wildly hoping that the news might somehow be better if it came from the horse's mouth.

'He's in theatre again at the moment. I can try and find a time for you to speak to him. I'm afraid he won't be able to tell you a great deal more than I've told you already.'

'Does he know?'

'Your husband? We leave it up to the families to decide whether patients should be told or not. Can I get you a cup of tea or anything?'

'No.'

'It is only a month. He won't have to suffer long. He's recovering from the operation now, but it wasn't a very long one, you can take him home the day after tomorrow. Are you sure I can't get you a cup of tea.'

'No.'

And that was it. The sister ushered us out. It was one more unpleasant job for her, no doubt, among many. My mother remained stunned as we drove back in the car. She broke down when we got home. I held her and tried to calm her and sat her down and went and made tea. The house felt unfamiliar already, as if a deathly quiet had fallen on it that made the ticking of the clock and the bubbling of the kettle unnaturally loud.

'I can't tell him,' she said gripping a handkerchief between her hands and staring at the carpet.

'I think he ought to be told.'

'I can't tell him. Why do they put this on you? Why can't they do it? They're useless!'

'I suppose they think it's better if it comes from …'

'How can I sit here and say to him "you're going to die". He didn't even get a proper retirement. Poor Don!' She broke down in sobs again.

'Perhaps he knows already, in his heart of hearts …'

'They told him the last time he was going to be all right. They told him this time it was just … It's not fair. A month! What if he doesn't know?'

'We have to tell him.'

'You mean I'll have to tell him.'

'We're not going to leave you alone to cope with this.'

'You're a good boy. He thinks the world of you, you know that, you and Dave. It's so unfair.'

'Your tea's getting cold.'

'I don't want bloody tea! I'm sorry, I'll get over it. I must. I can't spend his last month bursting into tears every time I see him. Poor Don!'

Then we just sat in silence for a while just trying to get used to the new reality. I couldn't really take it in. I got up on the pretext of going to the lavatory. In the bathroom, my father's shaving things were neatly arranged on a shelf above the washbasin. My old room had been rearranged as a guest bedroom and the view from the window was slightly different because new houses had gone up behind ours. To me it still seemed impregnated with my life as it had been when I lived at home. It was not that memories came flooding back; there was just the sense that I had been there and there was a connection, but the connection made no real sense now. I did remember how when I was very small, my father would slip quietly into the room when I was asleep, or supposed to be asleep, and make the sign of the cross over me and over Dave, who didn't then have a room of his own. He was a father, a protector, a comforter, and a generally dear presence taken for granted. This was what I hoped I would be for Annie. I realized also, with a pang, that our adult relations had not been that close and that one month was scarcely time to re-establish any sort of intimacy. Finally, as he was still a devout Christian man, I knew that there should be an aspect to his dying that went beyond physical pain and dissolution, but I also knew that I could not make any connection with that either. Someone else would have to bring God into it, I could not.

In order not to break down in tears myself, I went downstairs again and made more bloody tea.

My mother seemed to be in a trance, but when I urged tea on her again, she took it and it did seem to revive her a little.

'Shouldn't you be getting back?'

'I'll stay if you want me too.'

'No, I'll be all right. You've got your own family to take care of.'

'Is there anything you want me to do? Shall I ring, Dave?'

'No, I'll do that.' She said it calmly and with a sort of determination. I felt from that that, hopefully, she would be all right.

And revealing the truth to my father was not in the event as traumatic as she feared. Dave, my mother, and I went together to fetch him home. He looked terribly frail and was taken out to the car in a wheelchair, which we were allowed to take back with us packed in the boot. He sat in the back seat beside my mother with blankets round him. Dave drove, with me in the passenger seat. As we got clear of the hospital and turned into the main road, Dad turned to my mother and asked 'How long have I got?'

She swallowed very hard and we all tensed ourselves. 'A month,' she said.

He looked out of the window. 'Just my luck,' he said. 'Bloody February!'

* * *

He lasted long enough to see the first daffodils come out. In comparison to what I have heard from others who have watched people die of cancer, he, and therefore we, had a relatively easy time of it. For three weeks or so he was able to move around slowly and sit, as if he was simply taking things easy in order to get better, but his skin took on a yellowish tinge and he tended to fall asleep at the drop of a hat, sometimes more or less in the middle of a sentence. We tried to keep a semblance of normal life going on around him. I went over with Bea and Annie as often as I could. I hoped Annie might retain some recollection of him, though she was still too little really. She was toddling and beginning to string words together. She would say 'granddad read' and bring a book over and deposit it in his lap. I would hitch her up to sit on the sofa in the crook of his arm so that he could read to her, but she was too active to sit still for more than a few minutes, jabbing her finger at the pictures and saying 'what that?'. Then she would be squirming away to go and play with her toys on the floor or search for grandma in the kitchen.

There were so many things I should have liked to talk to him about, If, say, there had been a year to go, I would have tried to fill in some the gaps in my knowledge of the family history as far as back as he could remember, in addition to trying to get to know him better, at last, as a person. But we were stuck where we were. I had one conversation with him that seemed of some significance. On an unusually fine and warm day, he asked if I would take him out a little way in the wheelchair. I wheeled him down as far as the river, a place where we had been taken often as children to feed the ducks. The low sun was shining right in our eyes and spreading a shimmering carpet of gold over the water.

'Perhaps it will be like that,' he said.

'Where?'

'Where I'm going. I'm sorry you don't believe. It is a hope, you know, it is a comfort. And if it's a vain hope, I shan't know anything about it. That's a comfort too. Would you mind turning me a little, the sun is very bright.'

'I shall miss you.' I said, swivelling the wheelchair round.

'Not too much, I hope. You seem happy, are you?'

'I am — not at this moment; I mean, generally.'

'Well you should be, you have a beautiful wife and a beautiful daughter. There is more …' He drifted off. I waited, staring at the water, in case he should wake up again. In a few minutes, he did.

'Was I saying something?'

'You said "there is more …"'

'More what?'

'I don't know.'

'I wish sometimes there had been more of everything. Perhaps that's what I meant.'

'Do you wish that?'

'More … I was born with too tight a skin. If I could take it off and step outside it, I would be more … myself. Well, perhaps, I shall be. All those journeys back and forth to London, day after day, ah well.'

'You did what you had to. You were a good husband, a good father, a good man.'

'Thank you, dear boy. You see, I would have liked …'

And there he drifted off again and this time he didn't wake up until after I had pushed him back to the house and been scolded by my mother for keeping him out too long.

That was my last conversation with him that was not about ordinary matters. Soon after that he became too weak to get out of bed. The doctor and a nurse came regularly to help my mother. Then he lapsed into unconsciousness, but it took him a further week to die. It was as if death or the disease was gradually cutting the vital linkages one by one, but it was not a clean orderly process, it was brutal and brutish. While he had been conscious and himself, he had been mild and resigned. Now he was unconscious, his laborious breathing and occasional spasmodic movements suggested something violent was going on. But we told ourselves he was unconscious, he could not feel anything, and the doctor assured my mother she was giving him things to keep him 'comfortable'. Someone was with him in the bedroom — my old room again — most of the time. Once, when I was on watch, he cried out 'I can't, I can't'. I sprang up from the chair I was sitting in and rushed over to the bed. But there was nothing I could do, except hold his hand. He subsided again into the same pattern of laboured breathing. It was not the final moment. He died one afternoon while I was on my way home from work. Bea took the call and I immediately got into the car — my father's old car borrowed to make these journeys — and made my way out there.

I went to look at him. Even the dead who have died in bed do not look peaceful — that must be work of the undertakers. There may be peace around them, but their bodies look as if they have just been through a losing fight, and been thrown down and discarded as too wretched and pitifully ugly to endure. I do not care to remember my father that way, though the image will not entirely go away. I kissed the disfigured husk of him on the forehead. The undertakers arrive shortly afterwards and took him away. It was over.

At least it was over. My mother, who was exhausted after all the strain and laying awake or sitting up many nights, went straight to bed. Dave and I sat downstairs and drank our way through the remains of a bottle of whisky, talking very animatedly and even laughing because the tension was off, and we had, I suppose, come through.

16

After the funeral things gradually returned to normal. My mother stayed with us for a week, but wouldn't be persuaded to stay longer, because, as she said, she wanted to get her life back in order and she had to get used to being on her own. Her house might be full of painful memories, but she had plenty of friends locally and plenty to do.

Bea, in the meantime, who had been very supportive throughout this difficult time, had discovered her true vocation.

Having read her way through large portions of English and world literature since her first coming to live with me, she had decided, after Annie's birth, that one form of creation leads naturally on to another and that she ought to give back some of what she had taken in, and that if X, Y, and Z — who patently had less brain than earwax — could do it, then so could she. During Annie's afternoon naps, she had begun writing a novel — without telling me, in case, as she said, the results were just too embarrassing or she simply didn't have the stamina to bash out the required number of words.

Taking her cue from a friend of hers who had tried the same thing, Bea's first effort was aimed at Mills & Boon and written in accordance with their formula. It was entitled *American Serenade*. It told the story of a young woman called Trixie who has long blonde hair and a wonderfully sweet nature, but, alas, a mouth of slightly overgenerous proportions and a few too many teeth. While working as a waitress in a diner in Santa Monica, Trixie accidentally drops a plateful of eggs Benedict into the lap of a darkly handsome, widowed American industrialist of Italian extraction. Thereafter, the usual complications are followed by the usual end result. Bea was sufficiently happy with what she had written to submit it, still without telling me or, as far as I know, anyone else, except possibly the friend who had passed on the style sheet from Mills & Boon.

The return of the typescript with the usual polite note 'We get many hundreds of submissions … etc, this shows considerable promise … etc, but … etc, etc' prompted her to throw the typescript into the bin and go into a lengthy sulk. When Bea was in a mood, my usual practice was to try and jolly her out of it, then, if that didn't work, to tiptoe around her, remove any cause of nuisance, and generally treat her like an unexploded bomb. A period of obvious avoidance would usually cause her to explode, which would usually clear the air and bring to light the original cause of her displeasure. That was what happened in this instance. She confessed to what she'd been up to, showed me the rejection letter, and I rushed straight out to retrieve the typescript before the dustmen arrived. After a show of reluctance, she agreed to let me read it — which I did, and I agreed with whoever had read it for the publishers, it did show promise. I suggested that she should write a real novel, or at least one that wasn't tied to a formula. She said that was what she really wanted to do, but thought it was probably easier to get published if she followed a standard formula — and anyway she wasn't sure that she had it in her to write. I countered by saying that she could do anything she wanted to if she put her mind to it and, moreover, if anyone had material in their life that would form a good basis for fiction then she was that person. I meant her past life, of course. I wasn't terribly enamoured of the idea her writing about us.

By this time, Annie was no longer obligingly going down for naps, but she was old enough to go to a playgroup for a couple of afternoons a week. Bea put her Amstrad in the back bedroom, which she now set up properly as a room of her own. She reworked some of the material from *American Serenade*, made her heroine Trixie (who retained the blonde hair and the teeth) into a hard-bitten, cynical, opportunist who deliberately deposits eggs Benedict over the smartly trousered private parts of a mobster, and is then forced to lick them off at gunpoint, threw in bucketfuls of graphic sex, wrote in a throwaway staccato mid-Atlantic style, and called the whole thing *California Scheming*.

Like someone who really means business, she had already begun a second book — which was to be a thinly disguised account of life at Hell Hall — when she was invited out to lunch by the literary agent to whom she had sent *California Scheming*. We agreed that it had to be, it absolutely had to be a good sign if you were invited out to lunch. She dressed to kill, left Annie with Mary, and took a taxi into town. When I got home, earlier than usual, there was nobody there, just a message on the answerphone to get round to Mary and Jimmy's place as soon as possible. I was slightly anxious in case anything had happened to Annie, but when I got there I found Bea, Mary, and Daisy well into a second bottle of champagne. Bea stood up, spread her arms wide, said 'come here!' and planted a big wet alcoholic kiss on me.

'How does it feel to have a wife who's the toast of literary London?' asked Mary.

'What happened?' I asked. 'Did he like it?'

'He loved it. He loved me. He loved everything. I'm the biggest thing since Joan Collins.'

'Jackie Collins,' prompted Daisy.

'Whoever! He was … *wetting* himself. Advances burble burble, American rights burble burble, film rights burble, burble. I'm going to be so big.'

'Big in Hornsey *and* in Crouch End.'

'Big everywhere!'

'Just like you were at the wedding!' said Mary, which had all of them wetting themselves.

'We want to know why you're all laughing.' said Mary's eldest George, who appeared at the kitchen door at the head of a small posse of children, including Annie.

'Because Bea's going to make lots of money,' said his mother.

'Is that funny?'

'Terribly funny. Why don't you all run along and play for a bit longer, we'll sober up in a minute. Go on.'

As the posse made its way back towards the play room, one little girl turned to Annie and said, 'Your mummy's going to be rich.'

And she was quite right, though it took a little time.

***

When we got home and had put Annie to bed, Bea gave me a bit more detail of what the agent had said. He was tremendously excited about the book. He loved the title, he loved the story, he thought there was a very good chance it would be made into a film. The only thing he wasn't too keen on was the name of the heroine — Bea had originally called her Trixie in a veiled reference to herself, of course. But the agent didn't like Trixie. He said it reminded him of fairies or good-goodies. He told Bea he wanted something more subtle, but at the same time more obvious ('if you see what I mean'!). He said the name was tremendously important because he could envisage a follow-up — in fact possibly a whole series of books based around the same character. We racked our brains for a bit, went through all the babies' names books we had and the name Bea came up with in the end was Meena. That seemed pretty obvious in one way and quite subtle in another. It was a name Bea felt she could sell to the agent and to the public. Mission accomplished! We racked our brains a bit more about who could possibly play Meena when the thing was filmed, then went to bed.

The agent was as good as his word. Bea received a handsome advance for her first novel and a contract to write two more Meena books. She put the Hell Hall saga aside to concentrate on Meena II. Annie spent more time at the playgroup. The Amstrad was replaced by a top-of-the-range PC. *California Scheming* came out and was somewhat snootily reviewed, but sold in large quantities, appeared at the lower end of the bestseller lists and began to move inexorably up. Soon it was being trumpeted as a hit. Bea started to do the things expected of a successful author. She sat in Waterstone's and signed copies. She appeared on radio, first on a book programme and then on *Woman's Hour*, and her self-confidence, her wit, and her occasional bouts of outrageousness made her a media natural. My mother began to be a quite frequent visitor to look after Annie. After Bea had been over to the States for the book's American launch, we began to think seriously of getting an au pair or a nanny. The money seemed to keep rolling in. Meena mark 2, entitled *California Whirls*, somehow got finished amid the melee. Then Bea found she was pregnant again.

Her timing probably could not have been much better. She could afford to take a break while *California Whirls* was going through the production process. By now we could easily have afforded to have decorators in to do up the house, something, as I mentioned before, that we had neglected to do when we first moved in, but she elected to do it herself again. She wanted a bit of peace, a bit of calm time to herself. Of course, things were not exactly as they were before, because she had to keep her career ticking over, write a page or two of Meena III when inspiration struck her, go on radio or television when asked, dash off the occasional review for a newspaper or magazine. There was always Annie, now three, to be thought of as well. I was pleased and touched, however, that she should hark back in this way to the way we had been. In the event, she only managed to do about half the house herself and we got professionals in to finish the job, but that was a detail.

My own career was proceeding at a less spectacular pace. The business encyclopaedia was finished and because everyone thought I had done a pretty good job on it and it got a good press in most of the business magazines, I was given a pay rise and put in charge of a new and much bigger project, a general encyclopaedia of the twentieth century, which was scheduled to come out in the mid-1990s and tap into the general sense of nostalgia and historical significance that would be generated as the century drew to its close. The Soviet Empire was falling apart. There was a general sense of hope and optimism abroad. People were talking about a new world order and an information age. We were thinking of electronic media as well as print. This looked like a genuinely big and exciting project, and I was out of the clutches of the business world as well. Though it was not spectacular progress, it was definitely progress. I threw myself into the preparatory work with relish.

Our second child, another girl, Imogen, was born at the end of February 1990, a few days before the second anniversary of my father's death. There was no question, unfortunately, of Bea being able to take things as easily as she had done with Annie. She was under pressure to get on with Meena III. Assuming that Imogen proved to be a quiet baby, it seemed not impossible that, once she had recovered from the birth, Bea would be able to establish a routine not unlike the one she had got into when Annie was very small and she was writing her first book. The difference between then and now, however, was the presence of an active three-year-old in the house. We increased the hours Annie spent at playschool and evolved a complicated routine in which I took Annie to school in the morning and Bea or one of her friends or one of her friends' au pairs collected her in the afternoon, and my mother acted as general back stop. Everyone said that we needed — Bea needed — domestic help of some description. But our house, though a nice house in a nice area, and now a smartly decorated house as well, was not particularly big. We had moved after the first baby, it seemed that we ought to move again after the second. House prices, after seeming to be on an upward course to infinity, had faltered. It seemed to be becoming a bit of a buyer's market for once. If we could sell our own place, it appeared possible that we might be able to pick up a larger one relatively reasonably, for it was the properties towards the higher end of the market that were starting to prove more difficult to shift. Not that we were short of money. We could have lived, just about, on my salary and a lot of the money that Bea was amassing from royalties and the sale of various rights to her books was simply sitting there, waiting to be spent on just such a move.

The only question was, where should we move to? Over the years I had lived there, I had grown rather attached to our corner of London. I knew my way around. I knew the local people, the shopkeepers and tradespeople, and felt that they knew me. I was local. I had roots, not the sort of roots you get by being born and raised in a place, but rootlets at least. Moreover, getting into and out of work was not a great problem, and I was familiar with the vagaries of all the tube and transport services. Most important of all, however, most of our friends lived not too far away and our best friends lived within walking and baby-buggying distance.

Bea was not entirely of the same mind, however. While not exactly what you would think of as a country girl, she wasn't particularly fond of London or of cities in general. Despite her peculiar relationship with her parents, she had a deep sentimental attachment to Hell Hall and its environs. It had been a settled home after several years of wandering during her father's army career. Later on, it had been the home she came back to on holidays from boarding school. In particular, she felt that London was not a good place to bring up children. Despite the fact that she got a lot of support and pleasure from her friends, she was strongly inclined to move out to somewhere at least periurban if not semi-rural.

Up to then, the fact that her mother advocated a particular course of action would have pretty well ensured that Bea would follow another, or the opposite, course. But relations between Hornsey and Hell Hall were beginning to change and improve. Both the Major and Mrs Williams were agreeably surprised and gratified that their daughter was turning into a minor celebrity. The former had always been a fairly frequent, but generally brief visitor; the latter had been a very infrequent one. As far as Annie was concerned, 'grandma' meant my mother, whom she saw every two weeks or so and who often stayed to look after her when Bea was away. Annie was aware, of course, that she had another grandmother, but Grandma Williams was someone she had to be reminded about, not someone she referred to spontaneously.

Now, about this time, Grandma Williams not only took on board the fact that she had a daughter who was making a name for herself as a writer, but also the fact that she had a granddaughter who had developed from a nappy-dirtying nuisance who created general disorder and babbled unintelligibly into a rather pretty and bright little girl whom one could talk to and do things with. Moreover, she decided that she was not going to be left out of this child's life — quite possibly, given the generally low opinion she held of the child's parents, she felt that she had a duty to be a significant influence on it. In fact, I think she may even have seen it in rather different terms as well — as a sort of battle of the grandmothers. She was damned if she was going to let this child's destiny be shaped by the Anderson family and its petty-bourgeois mentality. The Anderson matriarch had had her turn, now it was hers.

It certainly seemed to be in that spirit that she phoned up at the beginning of April.

'Nigel, can I speak to my daughter, please?'

'She's feeding the baby at the moment. Can I take a message or get her to call you back?'

'Can't you feed her for a change? There's something I particularly want to say to Beatrice.'

'I'm not equipped, Virginia. I don't have breasts.'

'That child should be on the bottle by now. Still, if Beatrice wants sagging bosoms, who am I to care? Tell her I want Anne to come and stay with me for a few days over Easter. You can bring her down on Easter Saturday. I expect Bill will be here.'

'Ah!'

'What?'

'I had actually arranged for us to go to my mother's on Easter Sunday and we were going to leave Annie ...'

'Hasn't your mother seen enough of her?'

'It's no hardship for her, and as she's on her own ...'

'I'm on my own most of the time. Anyway, you've never brought her down here to stay.'

'She hasn't really been old enough ...'

'She's stayed with your mother before, I expect.'

'She has, but ...'

'Why should Mrs Anderson get special treatment? And what has suburbia got to offer that's so special? Do you want Anne growing up not knowing what a cow looks like except from books? She'll love the dogs, and I've found a pony for her.'

'She's not old enough to ride.'

'You're the equestrian expert now, are you? Just tell Beatrice to ring me as soon as she's finished suckling.'

She had an unanswerable case really on the basis of fair do's for both sides of the family. Bea gave way easily enough, perhaps thinking she didn't want Annie and my mother to get too close — there are so many small jealousies where children and grandchildren are concerned. Come Easter, we drove down — we had gone from a no-car to a two-car family almost overnight — more than a little nervous at leaving our precious Annie to the mercies of her peculiar grandparents, to find that both of them were actually at the door waiting to greet the new arrival and that the back garden at Hell Hall had acquired a swing, a seesaw, and a large sandpit. Imogen was given no more than a cursory once-over, but they made a tremendous fuss of Annie. Phone calls during the week indicated clearly that she was having a wonderful time. The visit was extended beyond a few days to a full week and when I drove back alone to fetch her back, it was 'Daddy, come and see this' and 'Daddy, I did that' and, especially, 'Daddy come and watch me ride'. Annie in a small hard hat was paraded up and down a neighbour's paddock astride a very docile Shetland pony by her grandmother, who forbore for once to comment, but gave me several speaking looks.

After that there was one more vote in the family in favour of moving out of town.

So, to cut a long story short, it came about that by the spring of 1991 we were living near the top of a hill in the vicinity of Ryehamstead in west Hertfordshire in a large detached house of conservative, middle-twentieth-century appearance in middle England, which boasted a double garage and extensive gardens front and rear, and enjoyed easy access to the Chiltern Hills, a local riding stables, a middling famous public school (and its satellite girls' school and prep school and a number of unimpeachably middle-class kindergartens), and a reasonably quick commuter service in to Euston — not to mention being within an hour's drive of Heathrow. It was not quite equidistant between Hell Hall and Roxdon, but both were quite easily reachable by cross-country routes or by the M25 and motorways if preferred.

In these respects, it was an ideal location. We had no roots there and didn't know a soul when we arrived, but the vendors assured us it was a very friendly area with lots going on (and Aylesbury just down the road!). In any case, though Bea and I were both in our later thirties — Bea was staring the dreaded 40 in the face — we could still just about pass as a young family inasmuch as our children were still young. We had it all to do if we wanted to establish ourselves as part of the community, but we had plenty of time to do it. I confidently expected, nevertheless, that our social life would continue to be centred in London, mainly among the tried and trusted circle of friends we had built up there. This expectation proved to be false. Though we were only twenty-five miles away, those miles made it much more complicated getting together. People came and stayed weekends occasionally at the beginning, and Bea and I, separately or jointly, sometimes met up with people in town, but the easy sociability we had taken for granted became a thing of the past.

We also acquired an aged but very effective gardener called John, who came with the place and was about the only grass-roots local we knew, and an Austrian au pair called Inge.

This, then, was what our children were to know as their home. For Bea it fell a good way short of Long Island in terms of amenities and prestige, but she had the satisfaction of knowing that it was hers to run as she liked — also hers in a more basic sense: we could never have afforded it without her income. It was more than I ever dreamed of, I suppose — but that is not very relevant, since I hadn't spent much time dreaming about the sort of place I aspired to live in — beyond, perhaps, picturing myself in a large leather armchair in a book-lined space in something handsomely Georgian. I was aware that these Ryehamstead splendours were mainly purchased with Bea's money while, in an ideal world, I should have liked the investment to have been 50/50 — indeed, I occasionally found myself wishing I was still the main bread-winner. But Bea, at that stage, never harped on the fact that she had lifted us out of Hornsey and deposited us in Hill End, as our road was called. We two (we four) were still one; it was our house, our success. And if it ever crossed my mind to resent the fact that I no longer had the traditional male role, I could always tell myself that I had borne the labour and the heat of the day — I had given Bea her launch pad in one sense — and that her rewards were out of all proportion to the efforts she had put in, strenuous as those efforts often were. She had a bankable talent, which was her good fortune, and she had had the additional good fortune that people had spotted it. We plodders must be content to plod.

17

For the first year or so, things worked well enough. Bea carried Meena III through to completion; Inge looked after Imogen and took Annie backwards and forwards to kindergarten and later to pre-prep school. Bea was not keen to produce yet another volume of Meena's Californian saga (*Meena Goes to the Bathroom*? *Meena Gets Even Meaner*?), but agreed to write one more at her publisher's and agent's bidding when they waved a sufficiently large cheque under her nose and promised that she could kill her heroine off at the end of it. We spent a hilarious evening, first on the sofa then sitting up in bed, devising spectacular exits for the woman. I followed, *mutatis mutandis*, in my father's footsteps commuting back and forth to London every day, and drew some satisfaction from the fact that the great encyclopaedia had been planned down to the last detail, that contributors, some of them very distinguished people, had been secured to write the main articles, and the first of their contributions had begun to come in. The house at Hill End was considerably larger than our previous one and our furniture at first had a thinly sown look, but we gradually filled in the gaps with the help of an interior designer and by visiting auctions and antique shops, which was a pleasant activity in itself. We had Mary and Jimmy and their children over for a weekend, and some other friends too, and we met a few people locally, and I even found a couple of fellow commuters who were willing to talk on the way into or out of town occasionally, instead of remaining buried in their newspapers.

But then two things happened that began the process that changed everything.

* * *

Bea said she wanted another baby before her time was up, and she was specifically hoping for a boy. Neither of us was in any way dissatisfied with the two girls we had already and they themselves seemed to be developing into two different characters — Annie was the active, high-spirited one, who seemed to be very bright and curious, with a will and mind of her own and a tendency to fits of temper and petulance if she didn't get her own way. Imogen seemed to be a more placid little person. She had certainly cried less than Annie and given us fewer broken nights, though we couldn't be sure whether this was owing to a more docile nature or to the fact that we were practised parents with more skills, less tendency to panic, and greater patience by the time she came along. Nevertheless, when, a few months after we had moved into Hill End, Bea proposed that we 'try for a boy', I was very happy to go along with her. We had the space, we had the money — though times were hard for a lot of people in 1992 — and a male child (if we were lucky enough to have one) would make things complete. It was a terrible irony, as things turned out, that this would have been the first baby we had jointly 'planned' and jointly and actively set out to conceive.

We took a break in July and moved the whole family plus Inge to a villa in southern France with a swimming pool for a three-week holiday. Bea took along a notebook in case any brilliant ideas occurred to her, but otherwise it was to be a period of total relaxation, getting away from it all, and as much lovemaking as could be fitted in between bouts of supine idleness and large meals in local restaurants.

Sure enough, the desired result was achieved, and in early September she announced that she was expecting again. This was very happy news, though the happiness was not entirely unalloyed.

As I have said, 1992 was not a good year for a lot of people. I knew of companies that had gone bust, people who had lost their jobs, people who had posted the keys of houses they had bought at the height of the property boom through the doors of the building society because they simply could not keep up mortgage payments now that interest rates had risen so high. I was vaguely anxious, as most people were, but I knew we were not over-extended on the property front, despite our lavish new premises, because, thanks to Bea, we had not had to increase our mortgage greatly. Moreover, I was in charge of a prestige project that had been up and running for two years or thereabouts and in which a lot of work and money had already been invested. Relatively speaking, it should have been downhill all the way from this point to publication in early 1995.

I was right about the downhill direction, but not much else. I went back to work at the beginning of August reluctantly, but with a pleasant sense of having had a really good holiday and that, once the languor of sunny days had worn off, I would be able to get down to my task again with renewed vigour. I found a memo on my desk asking me to go and see my boss at 9.30. I assumed that she wanted to discuss the next stage of the project. I tried to focus my mind on it so that I had something convincing to say and did not give the impression that the encyclopaedia had been the last thing I had been thinking about over the previous three weeks.

I decided to pop in and have a word with one of my two assistants to get up to date with things — I knew the other was scheduled to go on holiday from the time I came back. Lisa wasn't there, and the office she shared with Charles, the assistant who was away, was empty. There were a few papers strewn over the desk and the rival encyclopaedias that we had to pilfer from, emulate, and outdo, were still in the shelves, but the computers had been removed and so had the filing cabinets that contained paper back-ups of the most important documents we were amassing.

This was odd; it was more than odd, it was distinctly disturbing. In fact it looked grim. There was still a quarter of an hour to go before my appointment with Julia, my boss. I thought the person most likely to be able to tell me what was going on was Kathy, our admin person. But as I set out to find her, Julia arrived. She said 'you'd better come with me straight away' and led the way down the corridor, striding out with her briefcase under her arm.

'Did you have a good holiday?' she asked.

'Yes,' I said, 'thank you. What's going on?'

She did not reply. She motioned me to sit down, then went through her arriving-at-work ritual of putting down her case, taking off her jacket, throwing the grounds from her coffee machine into a plastic bag, tying the bag, disposing of it in the wastepaper basket, and setting the machine to make a new brew. I waited in suspense. Finally she sat down and looked at me. We got on well; we weren't close at all, but she was a good person to work for, considerate and approachable. She looked away.

'There's no easy way to do this,' she said.

'Do what?'

'I'm sorry, Nigel, your project's been axed.'

'What? But ...'

'I know, I know. It's nothing you've done. The company's losing money ... the company's been losing a lot of money, something has to go.'

'But we've spent two years ...'

'I know. I did my best. There was nothing I could do. The decision came from the top.'

'But this is so short-sighted. We've already got most of the stuff — and it's very good stuff. Has anyone read any of the articles? It doesn't make any sense.'

'It makes business sense — at least it does to them. It was a prestige project, Nigel. It was never going to make much money, especially not in the short term. You knew that, surely.'

'No, I didn't know that. All I knew was … I thought we were genuinely putting together a really good book. It was the first thing I've ever done that I felt really proud of.'

'I know, I'm sorry. Nobody's questioning your commitment.'

'Is there any chance they might change their minds?'

'No. They decided weeks ago. They might try and sell your stuff on to another publisher, but it's unlikely anyone'll want it in the present climate.'

'How long have you known?'

'About four weeks.'

'Why didn't you tell me?'

'I didn't want to spoil your holiday.'

'Well, if it's possible to spoil something retrospectively, you have spoilt it. … Sorry. I realize it's not your fault. Bloody hell! All that work!'

'Do you want a coffee?'

'Not really. Is that it? What about me? Am I being shifted on to something else?'

'No.'

There was a silence while she allowed this to sink in.

'You mean, I'm being sacked?'

'We're having to let a lot of people go. I'm hanging on by the skin of my teeth. It wouldn't surprise me if they weren't keeping me on just to sack everyone else.'

'Lisa and Charles?'

'They've already gone.'

'But I … I had no idea. I've done my job. Nobody told me I'd done anything wrong, you've always said — everybody's always said …'

'It's not your fault!'

'Then whose fault is it?'

'It's nobody's fault. I'm sorry. The economy's gone to pieces. It happens.'

'Is there anything I can do about it?'

'There doesn't seem to be anything the government can do about it. Ask Norman Lamont.'

'I meant, can I complain, can I appeal, can I go and see anyone higher up?'

'No, basically. You've got your contract. You can work out your notice if you want to, but we'd rather — and I think, it's best for you — that you cleared your desk today and took money in lieu of notice. Kathy can tell you about redundancy and your pension and all that.'

'Today, but I've only just come back from ... God!'

'I'm sorry. I know it's a shock. I've done this to six other people already. You're still young, Nigel, and you're good. You'll get another job. And, let's put it this way, you'll be all right financially. Bea's still churning them out, isn't she? There aren't so many problems at that end of the market. Charles was in tears. They've just had their first baby, as you know. He's afraid they'll lose their house.'

So, I was luckier than some. Not that it was much consolation. Kathy told me how much redundancy I was due on top of my salary to the end of August and three months pay in lieu of notice, and gave me some leaflets about pensions and benefits and provided a cardboard box for me to put any personal things in that wouldn't fit into my briefcase. I packed up my case and box, said brief goodbyes to the lucky ones who were staying, and walked out into a brilliant summer noon wondering what on earth I was going to do with myself, though with the partial reassurance that I had the best part of four months on full pay to make up my mind.

18

Bea was fine about it. Outraged on my behalf, initially, she urged me not to take it lying down — wasn't there something the union could do? No, there wasn't anything the union could do — except to offer sympathy and send out more leaflets about retraining or reskilling or discovering and making use of one's transferable skills. I wasn't sure I had any of those, having been in reference-book publishing for the whole of my working life. Lying down was a major part of taking it. I no longer had to get up early in the morning and get myself down to the station before the rest of the house was really stirring. It took a while to get myself out of the habit of waking up to the alarm clock at a quarter to six precisely every morning.

I started to get some idea of the routine of the rest of the household — though, as Annie was still on holiday, they weren't yet back into the full-blown version of that. Bea would lie in bed listening to the *Today* programme from about seven and get up at about eight. By that time, on a normal day, Inge would have got the girls up and be giving them their breakfast. Somewhere between nine and half past Bea would retire to her study and write until lunchtime. That was strictly her time; she was not to be disturbed by anyone, including me, except in cases of absolute emergency. While Bea was working, Inge would do a little housework — we had a cleaner who came in three times a week to do most of it — and look after Imogen. After lunch, Bea would write letters or make phone calls as required, then either play with the children, go out, or write a bit more until the late afternoon. Then, at the time when I had been accustomed to arrive home, everyone would gather in the kitchen for a bit of family time and to cook the evening meal.

It seemed like a very nice life and it seemed to run very smoothly. There wasn't an obvious role in it for me, though, as things stood. But then, why should there be? The obvious thing for me to do was to get myself another job. It being August and the middle of a recession, there was very little doing, but I tried to get into the habit of studying the adverts in the newspapers and the trade papers. I also wrote letters to, or rang, everyone I knew in the trade who might know of any openings. The results were not the least bit encouraging. Otherwise, I thought the best, and by far the pleasantest, use of the time I had on my hands was to devote it to the girls. We would get to know the local countryside. We had outings to the zoo at Whipsnade, to a theme park, and to some noted beauty spots. Everywhere seemed very crowded, but the children never seemed to mind very much unless it meant queuing for something for a long time in the heat. I remembered my family's old custom of Sunday afternoon walks and, for more peaceful jaunts, we would pack up a picnic and head out across country. I took a carrier to put Imogen in when she got tired. We found one particularly pleasant spot, not too far from the road, but far enough to deter anyone who wasn't prepared to walk for fifteen minutes to get there, by a bend in a small river where there was a gently sloping sandbank and the children could paddle in the clear, swiftly flowing water or try to catch minnows in a jam jar, or sit and watch the brilliant blue dragonflies hovering or flitting back and forth against the reeds on the opposite bank.

Bea seldom came with us. She was determined to get Meena good and dead and out of her life. The expeditionary force consisted usually of Inge, the two girls, and myself — though Annie had a life of her own too: she sometimes brought along friends of hers or went to spend the day with friends, and she was having riding lessons and piano lessons as any well-brought-up little girl should. One consequence of this was that I got to know Inge a good deal better than I might otherwise have done.

She was twenty, tall and quite strongly built with dark hair and a face that was pleasant, I think you would say, rather than pretty. She came from St Gilgen, a small lakeside town not far from Salzburg. Mozart's sister lived in St Gilgen after she was married, she told me. Not that she showed any great interest in Mozart other than as a national cultural icon. She preferred pop. She was in a completely different class to Jill's hapless Monique. She was very efficient about the house and very good with, and fond of, the girls. They seemed to be equally fond of her. The only fault I could find with her was that she was a bit pedestrian and did not have much of a sense of humour — but maybe that had more to do with the quality of my jokes or with language difficulties. Her English was reasonable but not brilliant.

Sitting by the river while the girls paddled or threw stone or twigs into the water, she told me more about herself and her plans.

'I spend two years in England to learn English, then I spend two years in Austria to make money, then I spend two years to go around the world, then I do something else.'

'What's the something else?'

'Who knows? Six years after, who knows?'

'Is there anything you want to do?'

She shrugged her shoulders. 'Annie, be careful. You hit your sister with that stick — I want to see the world. Maybe I get a job later. What do you want to do, Mr Anderson?'

'Call me Nigel.'

'What do you want to do, Nigel?'

'I want to get another job, but then I'm a boring old fart. Annie! Inge told you to be careful!' I went to retrieve Imogen, who'd been accidentally knocked over by her sister, and carried her back to where we were sitting. Imogen cried to be handed over to Inge to be comforted. Annie poked her tongue out at everyone and then wandered off to paddle in deeper water.

'What is a fart, Nigel? ...' I explained, laboriously. 'But you are not a boring foolish man, Nigel, I think you are quite nice. Is it all right to call someone a fart?'

'No, not when you're actually speaking to them.'

'You do not mind if I ask you these questions?'

'Not at all, you've got a lot to learn in two years.'

'My English is not good, I know. Do you think two years is not enough?'

'Your English is coming along fine. Just let her go back now.' Imogen was struggling to get out of Inge's arms and back to the action. 'If you took more than two years, you'd throw all your plans out.'

'No, I would not. I would keep my plan, but it would not be exact as I have thought.'

'No. I meant ... "throw out" means — can also mean — er — dislocate — dislocate your plans.'

'Please, "dislocate"?

'Make them different from what they were supposed to be — spoil them. Anyway, you're probably right not to think too far ahead. Six years ago I didn't think I'd be where I am now — I mean, I didn't think I'd have no job. And in another six years, as you say, who knows?'

'But Mrs Anderson is rich and famous. That is a good thing for you.'

'That's what everyone tells me. So long as she keeps churning them out, everything will be hunky dory.'

'Please, "churning them out"?

* * *

I was at home, therefore, when Bea made her joyful announcement that there would be five of us in the family from the following year. She was scheduled to make another promotional trip to the States at the end of October. I was a bit doubtful whether this was wise under the circumstances. But her agent and her American publisher were both very keen that she should go, she herself was feeling well, and she had not experienced any problems carrying the two girls. The doctor said that the danger of anything happening was considerably reduced after the three-months mark, so there did not seem any compelling reason to cancel the trip.

She might well have been glad to get away for a while in any case. I was probably not the best of company. Being unemployed was getting me down. I had written dozens of speculative letters and applied for anything that came up. But there was precious little to apply for. I was called to an interview with a publisher in Oxford. I knew they were interviewing at least five other people, and I ran into two of them, people I knew vaguely from meeting them at conferences or book fairs and the like. Both of them had more or less the same amount of experience as I did; one of them fitted the bill for the particular job on offer much better than me. I did my best at the interview to convince the elderly, tweedy man and the sharp-eyed woman who made copious notes that I would electrify their reference department and had a head teeming with brilliant ideas, while feeling far from confident that either of these was the case. When the news of my unsuccess was communicated by letter a few days later, I was not surprised. Nor was I surprised to learn subsequently, from the acquaintance I had spoken to briefly as I came out, that the post had been filled by internal promotion, so the whole interviewing exercise had been undertaken simply for the sake of form.

There was one other job that came up shortly before Bea left for America; it was based in Glasgow. When I asked her how she would feel about relocating to Scotland, in the unlikely event that I was offered something, she said 'over my dead body!' and told me in no uncertain terms that if I went, I would be going on my own. I didn't even bother to apply.

I moped. With Annie back at school, there was not much for me to do. I offered to help Bea, but she said firmly that she didn't need any help. I offered to help Inge, but she didn't need help either. I read the newspaper from cover to cover, I bought a few French and German paperbacks to try and brush up my languages, I went for walks, I tried to engage Bea in conversation whenever she showed herself outside her office — but she never really wanted to talk, she just wanted to get on with her book and make sure it was finished before the baby arrived. One day a week I came into my own, when Inge had time off. Then I got to ferry Annie back and forth, make lunch, and try to keep Imogen amused, so that she wasn't tempted to go and disturb her mother. I desperately wanted to be a good father in theory, but in the everyday, full-time practice of looking after a small child, I was only moderately successful. And, placid and sweet-tempered as she was, Imogen was not above winding me up by running, or pretending to run, towards Bea's office door the instant I took my eyes off her, knowing that if she got in, Mummy would come out and give Daddy an earful for not looking after her properly.

So I felt bored, inadequate, and superfluous to requirements — in common with most of my kind. I was marking time until life began again: until I got a job, until Bea finished the book, until the baby was born and we picked up our love life once more. I remembered Steve and Brian eight years earlier and would have been glad to go out and picket someone, except there was no-one to picket or complain to and there was not even the pinch of hardship or a sense of communal grievance to spur me on. I was lucky; I merely had to come to terms with being idle in comfort.

That was, ostensibly, what Bea and I had the row about as I was driving her to Heathrow to fly off to New York.

'You've got to get a grip,' she said, never one to mince her words. 'Living with you is getting to be a real drag.'

'It's not my fault,' I replied hotly. 'I didn't ask to be thrown out of a job. I'm doing my best. There isn't anything.'

'Well, don't take it out on me.'

'I'm not taking it out on you.'

'You are. I can feel the envy oozing out of you. It's so bloody typical. You really do hate the fact that I'm doing better than you.'

I stared at her with a sense of genuine righteous indignation. I was sure I had never said anything like that.

'Keep your eyes on the road. Just because you don't say it,' she went on, 'doesn't mean you don't feel it.'

'I don't hate the fact. Everyone keeps telling me how bloody lucky I am to have an inordinately successful wife, as if I didn't know it already.'

'Except that you can't bear it.'

'I don't want to end up being a kept man, no. Though God knows why. You never objected to being a kept woman.'

'I was not a kept woman. Christ, I'd never have chosen you to keep me if that's what I'd wanted to be.'

'Sorry. My mistake. It was Rich that was keeping you while you stuffed yourself with Dickens and Trollope. I was just paying the bills, which is all I've ever done.'

'It's all you ever wanted to do.'

'How do you know what I wanted to do? When have you ever given a moment's thought to what I wanted to do?'

'You've got so little ambition, Nigel, it would have been a wasted moment in any case.'

'Is that what you think of me? Is that what you really think of me?'

She stared out of the window and made no reply. I was really angry by this time and drove off the main road at the next convenient point intending to pull up somewhere and have it out with her.

'Where are you going? I've got a fucking plane to catch.'

'I don't care about your fucking plane. We're going to have this out now.'

'Nigel, get back on the road. Get back on the ...'

And she reached over as if to grab the steering wheel. In fending her off, I made the car swerve slightly and the front wheel hit the kerb. We were not travelling very fast, fortunately, but it gave us a serious jolt. She gasped and clutched her belly. I stopped.

'Are you all right?'

'No.'

I was extremely frightened and sat there tensely, half expecting some ghastly sign or symptom to manifest itself that instant.

She sat still for a moment as if she had a similar fear herself. Nothing happened. She looked at me with very big eyes.

'Don't ever, ever do anything like that again.'

'But are you all right?'

'Just get me to the bloody airport.'

I turned the car around, and we drove to the airport in virtual silence. When she had completed the formalities at the terminal, she told me brusquely not to wait, turned away when I tried to kiss her, and stalked off through passport control and into the airside waiting area without looking back.

19

I drove home in an anxious and chastened frame of mind. I hoped and prayed that no harm had been done. It was a relatively small jolt; she was wearing a seatbelt; she had seemed all right when we parted. As for the row, the significance of that faded somewhat in view of the fright we had had, but it was still disturbing.

We did not usually have rows. This may seem strange, inasmuch as pugnacity had seemed to be a defining characteristic of Bea way back in the days when RT and I had observed her from afar slugging it out with her boyfriend beside the lake or when, later on, she had been going hammer and tongs with RT himself outside a seminar room. By the time she and I got together, she had been in many respects a genuinely changed woman. She was calmer and maturer; she wanted different things, I thought, and those things were the same things that I wanted. I had always congratulated myself on the harmoniousness of our relationship; we saw eye to eye, we did not quarrel about money or the children or sex or the division of labour in the house or the other issues that couples are usually supposed to fight over. And if there was friction, then it was never serious and never lasted long. I would not have wanted to cross her, to be sure, but then the question didn't really arise because we loved each other.

But what if ... and this suddenly came into my head as I was slowing down to turn off the M25 ... what if the comparative peacefulness of our relationship stemmed not from some superior degree of mutual love and sympathy, but from the simple fact that Bea always got her way. A relationship between two people with strong wills and strong desires is almost bound to be tempestuous. But where one partner is strong-willed and the other weak ... if the one had no ambition beyond paying the bills ... I came back to myself realizing I had been driving on automatic pilot for several minutes, and tried to get a grip. I did not want to start thinking like that. We had had a row. It probably didn't mean anything. The best thing was to forget it. When Bea came back from America, she would probably have forgotten it. We would carry on as before — that is, as we were before I lost my job. I couldn't go on moping and being useless and a drag — she was quite right about that. While she was away, I really must get a grip on myself, and if I couldn't get a job — and I couldn't magic one out of thin air — then at least I must get myself organized in some productive way.

Except … she had said some pretty hard things to me, and these had come more or less out of a clear blue sky. When such things burst out during a quarrel, you often can't tell whether they are just angry words that come out of the immediate situation or whether they bring to light some deep-seated feeling or long-harboured thought that the utterer has previously repressed or not even been conscious of. It is possible too that they are essentially a challenge or a bait. Their main function, irrespective of their truth content, may be to get some sort of response out of the person they are flung at. I was quite willing to admit that I might have been a drag, even that I envied her success a little — though not in any way that I felt was malicious. But if she genuinely despised me as inadequate … I imagined her still sitting in the departure lounge waiting for her flight to be called, perhaps resolving that when she came back she would finish what she had started. She would call time. She would get rid of the impediment she had saddled herself with. I had served my purpose.

But this was ridiculous. We were happy, we had two children and a third on the way, we had built a life etc, etc. I was depressed and up to my old trick of analysing everything in minute and grisly detail. Get a grip.

I knew that in all probability she would ring home the following day before the children went to bed. It was Inge's day off. I made sure that I got up early and kept as busy as I could all day. Since the afternoon was reasonably fine, I packed Imogen into the car and carted her off, with the back carrier, to scale Ivinghoe Beacon, one of the highest points in the Chilterns, though not exactly Everest. I felt her little arms clasped round my neck and her breath on my ear, as I panted up this fairly modest eminence. We spent a long time pointing things out to each other, especially the white lion on the downs at Whipsnade; then we walked down again slowly hand in hand, until we were close enough to the bottom to run the rest of the way. Then I picked her up and swung her around, and tickled her. In the car on the way to pick up Annie and go home, she asked for a story and I concocted a tale about a white lion whom all the other lions said was a freak and who went to the lion doctor to get some pills to make him change colour ... I was just beginning to get into this, when I saw in the mirror that she had fallen asleep in her car seat. I told myself that I must make more of this time with the children. I would spend the next day, thinking seriously about that and about everything on which a grip could be got.

When the phone rang, I grabbed it immediately.

'Hello?'

'Hello!'

'How are you? Are you all right? Is everything OK over there?'

'I'm OK — a bit jet-lagged. You?'

'Fine. Trying to get a grip. Missing you.'

'Sure. How are the girls?'

'They're lined up ready to speak to you ...'

I gave the receiver to Imogen who just listened intently while her mother spoke to her without, as usual, saying a word despite frequent prompting, then said 'goodbye, Mummy' and handed the receiver to her sister. Annie prattled on about what she had done at school. When I felt she was running out of things to say, I gestured to her to pass the receiver back to me.

'Do you want to speak to Daddy again?' she said eventually. There was a brief silence, then she said, 'Goodbye Mummy, I love you too' and put the phone down.

'I wanted you to pass the phone back to me. What did Mummy say?'

'She said she's very busy and she'll ring again in a few days.'

* * *

There was no word from her for three or four days, then, in the middle of the evening, the phone rang. I picked it up and said 'hello?' – there was an eerie silence at the other end. I said 'hello?' again a couple more times and was about to put the phone down, thinking it must be some kind of crank call, when Bea's voice emerged sounding very hollow and distant.

'I've lost the baby,' was all she said.

'Oh no! Oh no! Are *you* all right? ... Bea, are *you* all right? ... Hello, Bea?'

She couldn't or wouldn't say any more. After a brief silence the phone went dead.

She had left two contact numbers, her hotel and her publishers. I frantically rang the hotel and asked for Mrs Anderson. They said they had no Mrs Anderson staying with them. I was forgetting that she wrote under her maiden name and presumably registered under it. I asked for Bea Williams. They said she had left that morning and hadn't returned yet, could they take a message? Her publishers said that she had come that morning for a meeting and had left before midday. They thought she was going to meet a friend for lunch. I told them what the situation was, as far as I knew, and they said they would try and find out more and would call me back as soon as they knew anything. I had visions of Bea collapsing in the street in the middle of an enormous, pitiless city. I had no idea where she had been calling from and could only hope it was a hospital.

I had to get to her. I told Inge what had happened and said I was leaving on the next available flight. I managed to get a seat on one leaving at noon the following day. I rang my mother and Bea's parents to put them in the picture and ask them to be ready to help out with the girls if needed. Someone from the publishers rang back at around midnight to say that they had located her. She complained of stomach pains at lunch and gone to the bathroom. When she didn't reappear, the person she had been lunching with had got worried. She had been found, an ambulance had been called, and she'd been taken to hospital. They gave me the number of the hospital and told me to come to their offices as soon as I arrived in New York and someone would take me there. I rang the hospital and they said she was sleeping, but that she was physically all right — it was 'a natural event' — and they were just keeping her in for a day or two for checks. I told them to tell her when she woke up that I would be there the following afternoon.

20

I found her in a comfortable, air-conditioned room that seemed to be full of flowers. There were two men visiting her when I arrived. Bea was sitting up in bed looking slightly pale but apparently in good shape and in reasonably good spirits. They all fell silent as I entered. After the stress of a hurried departure, the long anxious hours of the flight, and the tedious and frustrating business of getting through the airport, into town, and from the publishers' offices to the hospital, I felt immeasurable relief at finally seeing her and seeing that she seemed to be OK. My eyes filled with tears as I lifted her off the pillows and held her in my arms.

The two visitors made to go. One introduced himself as Jerome O'Reilly; he told me he was her literary agent for the US, the other was Antonio Perry, the lawyer whom I had met about eight years earlier over Bea's divorce. He looked at me curiously as we shook hands, then he leant over the bed and kissed Bea briefly on the lips before he left, saying that he would call the hospital tomorrow and drop by again if she was still there.

When they had gone, I sat down by the bed and took her hand.

'How do you feel?' I asked.

'Awful,' she said. 'It's my fault.' And she began to cry.

I went to hold her again, but she fended me off and curled herself forward, holding her head in her hands and weeping bitterly.

'It's not your fault. It is absolutely not your fault. It happens to hundreds of women. Bea, please ...'

Once again I tried to take her in my arms, but she threw herself back against the pillows and said 'Don't touch me!'

'I'm sorry,' I said, drawing back and sitting down again. 'Bea, I know how much you wanted this baby. I wanted it too. But we still have each other and the girls. It will be all right. You mean everything to me, you and the girls. It will be all right.'

She lay rigid, staring straight ahead, with tears streaming down her face.

If someone will not be comforted, or you do not have it in your power to comfort them, there is little you can do except wait for the storm to subside. I kept repeating the same reassurances and trying to show little physical tendernesses, but the grief in her was too fierce for her to respond to me or anything I said or did. I supposed that she had kept up a brave face in the presence of strangers, but that when I arrived she was free to let it all out.

I had said I knew how much she wanted this baby, but that had been obviously untrue. As it was not inside of me, linked to me, I could not know what it was like to lose it. The new baby was a wonderful idea, a wonderful prospect, and I had looked ahead to seeing it born and watching it grow like the others. And it was bitterly disappointing to have that prospect wiped out. But I had been too consumed with worry about Bea to have had time to feel very much for the baby. She must have felt it slipping out of her and been powerless to do anything to stop it going. That must be another order of loss entirely.

I sat beside her hoping that she would respond or let me in somehow to share her grief, but she did not. In the end I went to find a doctor and told her that Bea was extremely distressed. The doctor reassured me in turn and said that it was best if I left and gave Bea a chance to recover in her own time.

The publishers had organized for me to stay in Bea's room. I went to the hotel, had something to eat, and went up to the room feeling completely exhausted. It was strange being in what was obviously Bea's space — her laptop and her diary were on the desk, her things were in the wardrobe — but a space in which I had no part. I remembered all the flowers in Bea's room at the hospital. Obviously she had networks here, a side life — probably dating from way back before we were even an item — of which I had no real sense. This happens. I recalled how at my father's funeral, several people turned up who had been his colleagues and friends at work whom I did not know and whom, more to the point, my mother scarcely seemed to know either.

The telephone in the room suddenly rang.

'Hello?'

'Hello, who is this?'

I explained that I was Bea's husband.

'Oh, hi. Her husband? Well, well. My name's Saul Bensusan, a friend of Bea's from way back. Sorry, I didn't know she had a husband — apart from the great Guildersleeve, of course. Is she there? Can I speak to her, please?'

I remembered the name. I told him what had happened. He was very concerned and said that he would call in at the hospital the next day.

When I returned to the hospital next day, I was the first of a stream of visitors, including Bensusan. Bea seemed better. She responded appropriately to some pretty gushing expressions of sympathy and bore with patience the accounts of miscarriages suffered by a couple of her female visitors — or their very good friends. Word had got around that she did have a husband, another husband. Nobody appeared to have been aware of this. They all ritually hugged me and said they were glad to know me, and what a tragedy this was for both of us, and what did I think of New York City. I said this was my first visit and I'd only been there a day and had had too much on my mind to take anything in. 'My God! Your first visit? Where have you been?' Several of them launched into accounts of visits to London and recalled meetings with Bea there, though at what period of her life this was, I had no idea. It could have been quite a pleasant gathering, but for the fact that I had really no chance of talking to Bea privately and ascertaining how she was feeling.

At around lunchtime, the hospital staff ushered everyone out saying that Bea was to be taken for an examination, and that if everything was OK she would be kept in one more night and be free to leave the next day. An elderly couple — 'we were neighbours with Bea way back when' — took charge of me and, promising to get me back at the right hour for a late-afternoon visit, gave me lunch, and offered to show me the city. We did the Empire State Building and wandered along Broadway and Fifth Avenue. They were charming and very hospitable ... and I can't even remember their names. I got the impression that New York was impressively, even oppressively, huge, and frenetically busy, and looked just like it did in pictures, still or moving. They left me back at the hospital making me promise to call them next day, if I had any free time, so that we could do the Statue of Liberty.

Back at the hospital Antonio Perry was once again in attendance, sitting by the bedside holding Bea's hand and chatting easily with her. He had filled out a bit in the space of eight years and was starting to lose his hair. He was not a particularly good-looking man, slightly below average height and with a fleshy face, but he had that air of confidence and power that seems to come with being a lawyer. His whole manner seemed to suggest 'anything I want, I know how to get; anything that comes my way, I can handle'. He looked after himself too. His suit and shoes had a sheen of quality, his hands were carefully manicured, and he gave off a slight, sweet scent.

When he had left, with a scented kiss for Bea and an injunction to call him, and a scented handshake for me and another brief ironic appraisal, I suggested that we might try and call home just to let the girls know we were all right and coming back soon. Bea spoke briefly to my mother, who called Annie to the phone — Imogen was already asleep.

Bea cried again when she hung up the receiver and again brushed me away, but not with the same bitter intensity as the day before.

I thought it better to keep to practical matters, especially how and when we should get home. According to the doctor, there were no complications. What Bea needed was rest, basically. She ought not to do anything strenuous for a while, but there was no intrinsic reason why she should not fly. The doctor also warned me that the full psychological impact might not reveal itself for some time. It was decided that Bea would stay in hospital for one more night, that I would collect her the following day, that she would spend one day finishing off the business she had to come to New York for — which she promised could be done by phone from the hotel room — and we would leave the day after that. All I had to do was to fix the air tickets.

* * *

I fixed for us to fly home first class, both for the comfort and so that we should have a pair of seats to ourselves. I hoped that we might have time to talk things over on the way, so that we could present a united front to the girls and the future. But we both fell asleep soon after take-off and woke up only when they brought round a meal — I think it was dinner and I think we were somewhere between Iceland and Scotland.

Bea waved the steward away when he offered her a tray.

'You must eat something,' I said.

'I don't want anything.'

'Bea, we have to try and put this behind us … That's easy to say, I know, but …'

'God,' she said, 'you say such stupid ordinary things!' and she hunched herself into her seat staring out of the window.

'I'm a stupid ordinary person.'

'Yes, you are, you are. That's exactly what you are. Leave me alone.'

I shut up for a moment; she remained hunched in her corner.

'If you're still blaming yourself ...'

'Nigel, for God's sake, stop trying to make things better. You don't know ...'

'I know I don't know. That doesn't stop me wanting to help. This not just your ... loss, it's mine as well. But ...'

'It's my fault.'

'It's not your fault, they gave me a whole spiel in the hospital. It's a natural event that sometimes happens — they say it could mean there was something wrong with the foetus, it happens to lots of women, it is not your fault.'

'You don't know anything.'

'It could be *my* fault. I drove us into the bloody kerb on the way to Heathrow.'

I lowered my voice again, aware that a pair of aircraft seats is not a great guarantee of privacy.

'When we get home,' I said, 'we'll sort things out properly. I know I've been a pain in the arse since I lost my job. I tried to think things through in the first couple of days you were away — you were right in what you said on the way to Heathrow. I will get a grip. I just need you to be all right. Everything I have is bound up in you.'

She breathed a heavy sigh and looked at me at last.

'You were so wrong to trust me.'

'Why? It was the best thing I ever did to marry you.'

'If only ...'

'What? Look, if you've got something to tell me, please ... Did you not want the baby?'

'Of course, I wanted the baby. Things have changed, it's my fault.'

'Stop saying it's your fault. It's nobody's fault, unless it's my fault.'

'Nigel, will you please stop saying that.'

'But it's true.'

'No, it isn't bloody true. You don't know anything.'

'Then tell me. What is it? What's going on?'

'You would never know, would you? You would never, never know.' She said this in a curious tone, half pitying, half, it seemed, in contempt.

'I know things have changed. I know just recently you've changed towards me.'

'Oh, well spotted.'

'Bea, this is not funny, this is life and death. I'm sorry, I should never have started this. If there are things you don't want to talk about, if there are things you don't want me to know …'

'No. I don't think I care any more. I don't think I care.'

'About what? About me?'

'I did care for you a lot – and suddenly I see you as this ordinary little man. You see, it is my fault. And it *was* my fault — this — probably, not yours, not ever yours; you weren't the one fucking up hill and down dale with Antonio.'

* * *

When your whole body is seized by an icy numbness, when your heart and brain seem to cease operations for a spasm of time, when someone says such a thing fairly coolly, and probably premeditatedly, and giving the impression that they are handing you the key to a situation that has existed for a long time and that they have accepted and dealt with and that is a shocking revelation only to you — then it may be that you part company with reality for a while and go into a state like a dream where you are powerless to act, move or cry out. Something like that happened. It was also like having your ears blocked by pressure changes as the plane climbs or descends and remotely hearing sounds from somewhere outside the sphere of deafness in which you are temporarily imprisoned.

'You ... bitch!'

She shrugged her shoulders and turned away to look out of the window again.

'You wanted to know,' she seemed to be saying, 'you were asking for it, begging for it, well here it is, and much good may it do you.'

I could feel all the implications of what she had just said, for me, for us, for the children, as it were, hammering on the door of my consciousness, but I was unable or unwilling to let them in. I sat completely blankly, having to be reminded to fasten my seatbelt because the plane was about to land.

***

Inge was at the airport with both the girls to pick us up. The sensation of half-being and unreality did not disperse because there were other people to relate to. I hugged the children without feeling the hug, as if they and I were wrapped in some invisible insulating substance. Fortunately, the girls were more interested in Bea. She seemed to be completely self-possessed, responding to them naturally, holding both their hands in the back seat and reassuring them that she was better now, but that there would be no baby brother or sister for them.

'Why not, mummy?'

'Because the baby died inside me ...' She could not control herself at that point and wept. Annie held Bea's hand tightly between both of hers. Imogen started crying too. The three of them held each other and wept. Inge, who was driving, asked me to pass her a tissue. I did so, and then continued to stare ahead through the windscreen.

My mother was waiting for us at home. There was more weeping. The girls cheered up a little when Bea produced a couple of small presents for them from New York, the latest in sweaters and baseball caps. Gradually the tide of emotion ebbed. My mother asked me if I was all right. I said I was fine and went off to unpack … actually an excuse to be alone for a time. I sat on the bed, hoping some sense of normality would come back to me. Nothing. I mechanically took the clothes out of my bag and put them in a pile for washing or replaced them in drawers and cupboards. My mother came in to see why I was taking so long.

'Are you sure you're all right?'

'A bit jet-lagged probably.'

'It's terrible, I know,' she said, sitting on the bed beside me and putting her arm around me. 'She probably shouldn't have gone to New York, but it was just one of those things. She was more than three months, and before three months is the dangerous time. You mustn't blame her — but you wouldn't, would you?'

'No.'

'I lost a baby myself, so I know how she's feeling. It was before I had you. I was desperate for a while. I thought I'd never be able to have children. But at least you don't have to worry about that. The girls are lovely …'

And she went on to tell me about the things she and the girls had been doing while Bea and I were away.

We got through the day. I did not spend any time alone with Bea until we went to bed. I sat up in the bed, still feeling like a zombie. She got in, turned off her light, smacked her head into the pillow determinedly, and curled up with her back to me.

'What do you want to do now?' I asked.

'Go to sleep.'

'How long …?'

'Ages. What does it matter? Go to sleep.'

After a sleepless night, I was glad to take the opportunity of driving my mother home to get out of the house and away from Bea again. My mother said she was quite happy to go back on the train, because I looked so tired, but I insisted that I was fine.

We had been driving along for some time in virtual silence, when she said 'I've been thinking.'

'What about?'

'This may not be a good time to mention it, but I'm sure things will get back to normal very quickly and in fact I've been thinking this for some time. The house is really too big for me now that I'm on my own, and I don't get too many visitors, do I?'

I looked at her.

'That's not a complaint. I know it makes more sense for me to come to you rather than for all of you to come over to me … and Dave and Maisie don't come very often. Anyway, I was wondering if I shouldn't sell it and buy something smaller, a bungalow or something.'

'Well, if you think you'd be happier …'

'I think I might be. It is a lot of work … and I might live another twenty years, who knows?'

'Have you seen a bungalow you'd like?'

'No, I haven't got that far. You see, I had such a happy time with the girls — I always do — and I've always got on so well with Bea — thank God you found her, do you remember what it was like when you were living on your own in that pokey little flat in Crouch End? I know you've got an au pair — and you've been lucky there too — Inge's very nice — but I could still be useful, because she has her days off and anyway you won't necessarily want the expense of an au pair when the girls get older. Anyway, I was thinking it would be much better for everyone if I was nearer. I know places are very expensive around here, I mean your area, but a house just like ours went for one hundred and twenty thousand just last month — can you imagine it? Your father and I bought ours for ten. Anyway, what do you think?'

'I … Wouldn't you miss your friends?'

'Yes, of course I would. But I could make new ones. There must be a WI or a Townswomen's Guild in Ryehamstead, I mean it's that sort of place, isn't it? And though I miss your father very much, I have to move on. I mean I have moved on because I do all the domestic things he used to do like paying the bills. Geoffrey — you remember Geoffrey, the vicar? He still remembers you — said we all have to move on. I mean I'm never going to do a great deal in my life except move out of one rut into another rut, but I should like to see a bit more of things before I die, even if it's only Hertfordshire instead of Essex. ... But you don't think it's a good idea.'

'No, I ... It's not a good time.'

'No, no, I suppose it isn't. And you probably wouldn't want an aged P living on your doorstep.'

'It's not that, Mum. Things are difficult.'

'Well, I know, with you being unemployed on top of all this. I shouldn't have mentioned it. Only I'm not going to do anything absolutely geriatric like going to live in Bournemouth and collect seashells. That's what your father had in mind, but he liked the seaside much more than me. I'm sorry; I'm distracting you. Look out, there's a car ... sorry. You have to learn to keep quiet when you're old.'

'You're not old.'

'But I still have to learn to keep quiet.'

'No, you don't have to ... There could be problems.'

'I know, darling, but there are always problems about everything. I think it's a good idea ... but I won't worry you about it now. Look at that maniac! People like that shouldn't be on the road.'

So it went on until we reached our old house. I went in to have a cup of tea and a bite to eat before setting off back again. It was evident that my mother had been seized by some sort of urge to change things, because she had shifted all the furniture around in the living room, had had the kitchen redecorated and some new cupboards fitted, and had painted the bathroom lilac.

I asked her if there was anything I could do for her while I was there.

'No, no, no, I'm fine. Didn't you ought to be getting back soon anyway? It gets dark so early, now the clocks have gone back.'

'Yes,' I said wearily. 'I suppose so.'

'Darling, are you sure you're fit to drive? You look absolutely worn out. If it didn't mean leaving Bea on her own, I'd suggest you stayed here for the night and went back in the morning.'

'I don't expect she'd miss me.'

'Well then, stay … Nigel, … Nigel, is there something wrong between you and Bea?'

'Mum, I don't know. I can't talk about it.' I got up to go.

But she stood in front of me and, in the way I remembered from way back, took my face between both her hands and looked hard at me.

'Is it about more than the baby?'

'Yes.'

'Is it serious?'

'Yes, Mum, please …' I took her hands away from my face, but she continued to look at me intently as if trying to project her concern and resolution into me through my eyes.

'You must sort it out. Whatever's happened, for both your sakes and for the sake of the girls, you must sort it out.'

'I will, I will.'

'You've got a wonderful marriage and two lovely children, you mustn't let anything spoil it.'

'No.'

And then she let me go, with an injunction to drive carefully and to ring her as soon as I got home to say that I was safe.

21

The light was failing and it had come on to rain as I started off homeward. To the general gloom was added the frustration of heavy traffic. But I was in no hurry to get back. I felt nothing except black misery: everything that had gone before was a lie, what lay ahead would be simply pain, anger, humiliation and an endless succession of joyless days with the burden of trying to sort things out and trying to keep things going for the sake of the children. I was aware of how short the time span was between things being all right and things seeming to be all wrong. At the same time I felt that the shortness of the time was irrelevant, a delusion almost. Bea's rejection of me had been so categorical ... that was what made me despair. The fact that she had been unfaithful ... well, I supposed that we could have got over that, because I supposed I still loved her and wanted to continue to live with her, even though I could get no access to those particular feelings at that moment. I had not intended to say anything to my mother and felt ashamed that I had, since all I had done was give her something to worry about without relieving my own distress. But she would have found out sooner or later, unless by some miracle I should arrive home to find that it had all been a bad dream or that then, or in the days to come, Bea would suddenly turn round and say: 'I've been a fool, I was out of my mind because of losing the baby, I'm sorry about Antonio, it meant nothing, absolutely nothing, the important thing is us.'

Though generally inclined, up to then, to assume that things turn out all right in the end, I was not so stupid as to think that a very likely outcome. Even when I got through the traffic and out onto the country roads, I continued to drive slowly to put off the moment of having to walk through the door and face Bea's coldness or the necessity of putting on an act for the benefit of Annie and Imogen. On top of this, I was feeling tired from the flight and the emotional drama of the past few days. I lowered the window to let the rain come in and turned the radio on loud to keep myself awake. The most glorious music came flooding out of the speakers. Its leisurely progression and slow build-up to thunderous crescendos said Bruckner, and by the time it got to the second movement I was able to identify it fairly confidently as his seventh symphony. I was quite close to Hill End now, but listening to music seemed greatly preferable to facing it at home. I pulled in to the side of the road about a hundred yards short of our drive and turned off the headlights. I was hoping that the music would give me strength, I suppose. Art can energize and art can inspire but, when the symphony finished and the applause in the concert hall faded, I cannot say that I felt less trepidation about the future or more confidence in my ability to handle it. But the music took me out of myself for a while and gave me a sort of reassurance: I could respond to it, so I wasn't emotionally dead; great things continued to exist in the world, even if it was a sodden dark miserable world where people betrayed and belittled each other. I felt I ought to try and keep hold of that.

* * *

I entered the house warily. Inge was the only one still up. She told me that Bea had gone to bed. She had said she was feeling tired and depressed and didn't want to be disturbed. I looked in on the children, who were both fast asleep, then sat with Inge watching television until she went to bed too. After hesitating for a while, I decided it was probably best to go and sleep in the spare room.

The regular routine went ahead as usual with Inge taking Annie to school and taking Imogen with her for the ride. I felt even more than usual that I had nothing to do — nothing worth doing — and that I must simply wait for Bea to emerge and see what her attitude was and take things from there. Inge returned from the school run and got busy in the kitchen; I played with Imogen. When it got to about half past ten, Bea still hadn't shown any signs of stirring. I went up and tapped on the bedroom door. There was no response. I opened the door and peeped inside. It was a grey day and the bedroom curtains were thick, so it was very dark in the room. She was still in bed apparently asleep. I assumed she was finally sleeping off the effects of everything that had happened in New York, and left her.

At about one o'clock I went to look in on her again. I asked her softly from the doorway if she was awake and if she wanted anything. Again there was no response. Again I left her. Inge asked if Bea wanted any lunch. I said that she still seemed to be asleep, and asked what had happened the day before. Inge said that Bea had spent most of the day while I was taking my mother home sitting in the study, that she had emerged in the early evening and spoken briefly to the children, said she wasn't hungry when offered something to eat, and that she had then gone to bed saying she was tired and depressed. 'Are you sure she's all right, Nigel?'

I went straight back upstairs with fear in my heart and opened the curtains. She was lying curled up tightly on one side of the bed. There was a bottle of vodka half empty on the floor beside the bed, and several empty packets of pain killers. She was still breathing. I shouted for Inge and rang for the ambulance. Inge came flying into the room. 'Try and wake her,' I said, at the same time trying to give details to the person on the other end of the phone.

We didn't know what to do. Shaking her had no effect. Inge thought of sticking her fingers down Bea's throat to make her vomit, but I was afraid she might choke on it. She was still breathing. Imogen came into the room. I told Inge to take her out again and go downstairs to let the ambulance people in, meanwhile shouting Bea's name and adjuring her to wake up and live.

Fortunately, the ambulance people arrived within minutes. They took one of the empty packets and told me to pick up all the foil containers and scattered pills and follow them to the hospital as quickly as I could in the car. By the time I arrived, they had already rushed her through and were in the process of pumping her out. I sat in a waiting area, clutching a bag full of pills. After what seemed an eternity, a doctor came out and asked 'Are you the husband?'

I nodded and got up. 'Is she …?'

'She'll be fine.'

I sat down again shaking all over. The doctor sat down beside me and took the bag.

'Are these …?' I nodded again. 'Well, she didn't take anything like enough of them to kill herself, luckily, if that's what she intended to do. I don't suppose you know how long ago she took them.'

'No.'

'Or why?'

I explained about the miscarriage and a little of what had been going on, and asked if I could see her.

'Give us a little while to give her a thorough examination and clean her up a bit. We'll have to keep her in for a while, but the main thing will be treating her depression. That sometimes takes a long time.'

He suggested I get myself a coffee and make any phone calls and they'd let me know when I could see her.

I rang Inge to tell her that Bea was going to be all right and to reassure the children. I then steeled myself and rang Bea's mother.

* * *

She blamed me, perhaps not surprisingly.

I was standing at the end of the bed looking down at Bea, who seemed to be in a deep peaceful sleep and perfectly as normal apart from her pallor, the hospital nightgown she was in, and the drip leading to her arm. Virginia came in and after contemplating her daughter for a few minutes turned to me and hissed in my ear: 'I will never ever forgive you for this.'

I said nothing. One small advantage of being still somewhat stunned was that I was temporarily immune to her poisons.

As we were leaving the hospital building for the car park, having been told again that Bea was in no danger and that we should come back in normal visiting hours the next day, Virginia returned to the attack.

'I'm taking the girls back with me,' she announced.

'No,' I said, 'there's no reason for that. They're perfectly OK at home, and Annie's got school.'

'They're coming with me. They need to get as far away from all this as possible — and from you.'

'I said that won't be necessary. I'm at home, and Inge's there to look after them as well.'

'I wouldn't trust you to look after a dog. You drove my daughter to this.'

'Virginia, you're talking nonsense.'

'I'm taking the girls with me.' And she stalked off to her car.

I walked quickly across to mine and drove straight off, having an uncomfortable feeling that if I allowed Virginia to make it back to the house first, she would have whisked the girls off before I could do anything about it. And of one thing I was certain: she was not going to have them. To let her take them would fatally weaken my position — quite what I meant by that I didn't stop to reason out — that was how the idea presented itself to me.

As I drove up to the hospital exit and stopped to wait for the lights to change, I glanced in the mirror and saw Virginia's big four-by-four nose up close behind me and come to a halt, revving impatiently, with its bull bars more or less up against my rear bumper. I set off as soon as the lights changed to turn right. As I did so, she roared past me on the inside of the turn, narrowly missing a car that was pulling up at the lights on the main road and forcing me to brake, then sped off in the direction of Hill End.

I had driven with her once or twice along country lanes — in even greater fear of my life than when driving with my father — and knew that behind the wheel of her designer tank she was utterly ruthless, indeed it was surprising that there were any road-walking pheasants or peasants left alive in her part of Wiltshire. Ridiculous as it was to indulge in these antics on a day when my wife had apparently tried to commit suicide, I got the bit between my teeth and thought 'right, you bitch, you don't know the bloody short cuts' and swung off the main road through the side streets to get up to a lane that eventually came out about a quarter of a mile past our house, keeping my foot as far down as I was able.

And I've no doubt the plan would have worked, if I had not got stuck behind a tractor. I hooted at him to let me pass and received a leisurely V-sign for my pains. By the time I was able to squeeze by, I was sure I would be too late. Still I screamed along the rest of the lane. By now I was in a kind of frenzy, interpreting her actions as an attempt to abduct my children. She was there before me, but her vehicle was still in the drive. I parked my car across the entrance so she could not get out and ran up to the house in something between blind panic and blind fury.

Fortunately, Inge hadn't let her simply bundle the girls into the car and drive off again, but had started asking questions and was now being roundly told what an execrable upstart foreigner she was in terms that, hopefully, her vocabulary didn't stretch to. The girls were holding hands and looking on wide-eyed as their grandmother urged them to go and get in her car. At that point, I burst in.

'Girls, you're not going with your grandma. Go upstairs, I'll call you in a minute.'

'Girls, get in my car!'

'Inge, will you please take the girls upstairs.'

'Don't touch those children!' She made a grab for them as Inge went to shepherd them away.

'Virginia, stop it!'

'I'm taking those children.'

'Leave them alone, you mad bitch, or I'll rip your bloody head off!' I grabbed her by both arms to prevent her going any further, as Inge finally managed to get them away upstairs.

Anyone who had looked in through the front window would have seen the completely bizarre spectacle of a man approaching forty screaming at a woman past sixty dressed in a tweed skirt and a Barbour coat, trying to restrain her, and sticking out his backside to avoid her attempts to knee him in the groin. Unseemly as this was, it is a sobering thought, that if I had tried to be my ordinary rational self, she would probably have walked all over me. It is much easier to resist the mad when you are mad yourself.

'This is the man that tried to kill your mother!' she shouted after the retreating children. 'Now he's threatening to kill me.'

'Right, that's it. Get out of my house.'

'Your house! Your house! You wouldn't have a penny, if it weren't for Beatrice. You useless piece of shit!' And she spat in my face.

I must have looked at her then as if I really might make good my threat to rip her head off, because I felt my whole body tense murderously and as I made a slight move towards her, she took an involuntary step backward.

'Virginia … you're going.'

'I'm not going without the children.'

'Yes, you are.' I took her by the arm and, ignoring her insults and ragings, marched her out to her car.

At that point she finally realized she was not going to get her way. She got into the four-by-four with a final venomous 'This isn't the last of this' and started the engine.

And at that point too I realized that my car was blocking the entrance.

She roared off as if she were going to grind it under her wheels, swerving past it at the last moment on the grass verge so that she merely dented the front wing and smashed the headlights, then disappeared at high speed down the road.

22

I got my disfigured car back up the drive under the eyes of a couple across the road, who had also seen the ambulance arrive earlier in the day. I fobbed them off with a 'my wife's been taken ill; my mother-in-law's upset' and left them to work it out for themselves. I dare say our stock went down in terms of respectability, but perhaps rose slightly in terms of entertainment value.

I did my best to explain things to the girls in a way that was supposed to make them seem less shocking: 'Mummy's ill again and had to go back into hospital, but she's going to be all right.'

'Is she really going to be all right? I want her to come home,' said Annie.

'Yes, yes, she is. She'll be home soon.'

'And why was grandma angry?'

'Because … she's upset.'

'Why is she upset?'

'Because she's worried about Mummy. Let's have something to eat now.'

'Grandma said you tried to kill Mummy.'

'Listen,' I said, sitting down and getting them both to stand in front of me. 'That is not true. You mustn't believe that. I wouldn't do Mummy any harm, I love her too much.'

I got them to sit beside me and put my arms around them and said: 'I'm sorry this has happened. You've got to be very good and very brave. When Mummy's better, we'll all be happy together again like we were before.'

After the girls had gone to bed, I sat down and suddenly felt completely drained, physically and emotionally. Inge came and sat with me. I got us both a drink. Even someone as placid as she was, could hardly fail to have been affected by the drama and upheaval going on all at once in what had up to then been a tranquil household.

She explained how Bea's mother had come rushing in demanding that the children leave with her immediately.

'I think this is not right. You have not said anything to me about this. Also I can see that she is very angry, very furious.'

'Yes well, thank you. Thank you very much for what you did today. I couldn't let the girls go with her. I don't think I'd ever have got them back.'

'No, this is not possible, is it? You are their father.'

'She's a law unto herself, Bea's mother — she … doesn't think anything's impossible if she takes it into her head to do it. And she hates me and thinks I'm completely useless, which doesn't help.'

'Why does she think that? It is not your fault that you have no job. Also you are a wonderful father and a good man. Since I am living here, I have thought this.'

'Well, thank you, but she thinks Bea should have married someone — I don't know, richer, more successful, more her kind of person. This goes back a long way.'

'Since all the time I am living here, I think that Bea must be very lucky — no, *glücklich*, happy — very happy that she has such a husband that cares for her. So why does she do such a thing?'

'I don't know.'

'You are a very kind man. You love her perhaps too much.'

I had never had this kind of conversation with Inge before. I suppose it was not surprising that she had got drawn into our family life, especially after the events of the last few days, and that day in particular. It was also gratifying to find someone who appeared to be sympathetic to me. There was so much I had to try and sort out, and that I had barely begun to get a hold on. It was very tempting to confide in someone.

'Thank you for saying so, but I don't think that's what she thinks … any more.'

'It changes things, this with the baby?'

'It has obviously depressed her that she lost the baby, and she seems to blame herself for it, so I suppose that's why she did it ... tried to kill herself.'

'But does she try to kill herself, do you think?'

'Well no, perhaps not, but that doesn't make it any easier to understand why ... Anyway, that's not all there is to it. There are other complications in her life.'

'Does she do such a thing before?'

'Not that I know of.'

'I ask you too many questions?'

'No, no, that's all right. I don't have enough answers, that's the problem.'

'It happens that people pretend to kill themselves. I have a friend who cuts herself' — she made a gesture of slashing her wrists — 'because a boyfriend leaves her. She does not want to die, just to make him feel sorry or come back to her.'

'Believe me, Inge, as far as I know I have never done anything to harm her, I love her, I have never said I wanted to leave her ... I'm sorry, I can't talk about this.'

I got up from the sofa, suddenly feeling that if I went on any further with the conversation I would break down in tears.

'What day is it tomorrow?' I asked, just to get back to matters I could handle.

'Saturday.'

'Is it your weekend off?'

'Yes, but I don't mind. There is nothing important I was going to do.'

'I'll have to go in to the hospital in the morning. I don't want to take the girls with me until I'm quite sure Bea's all right.'

'I think Annie has a riding lesson. I will go with Imogen, she likes to see the horses.'

'Thanks, and thanks for ... putting up with all of this.'

'That's OK. I will do anything for you, Nigel … I mean, you must not worry to ask me to do anything.'

'Thank you.'

I patted her on the shoulder. She looked at me very earnestly, and for a moment the need to be comforted, the need to feel some positive flow of emotion from someone was so great that I felt like taking her into my arms. But, for better or worse, the moment passed, and I turned away to bed down in the spare room again alone.

* * *

Bea was let out of hospital after a few days. She came home with a prescription for antidepressants and a schedule of weekly appointments with a psychiatrist at the hospital. I was told that she had already been started on the pills, but they took a few days before they began to have an effect, and that I needed to watch her carefully and, above all, ensure that she took her medication as she was supposed to.

It was fortunate that I was at home, because otherwise, I suppose, there would have been no way of preventing Bea's mother from getting in on the act, which she was still trying to do, ringing up frequently in an attempt to persuade either Bea or the girls or preferably all of them to move to Hell Hall. Inge, bless her, took to answering the phone most of the time to screen out Virginia's calls and take the flak when it came, answering the abuse with imperturbable, stilted politeness. She was also very good at insisting that Bea got up in the morning at a reasonable hour, ate regular meals, sat with us in the living room, and gradually began to take on small tasks. If left to herself, Bea might well have spent the whole day curled up in the foetal position in a darkened room. If it had been left to me to keep her going I don't know where I would have found the strength to overcome the resistance expressed in her hunched body and expressionless face. On the basis of the last things she had said to me, I took all that as being directed specifically at me. No doubt this was not really the case. Her withdrawnness was symptomatic of her depressed condition, not of her attitude to me, but her passive and sometimes active refusal to move always seemed like a barrier that it would take some kind of rough force to overcome — and any the least force from me would, I felt, have provoked an uncontrolled outburst from her. Inge, on the other hand, was able to treat her like a nurse, with the kind of sympathetic but impersonal firmness that was needed.

And gradually Bea began to recover. The first time she emerged from the bedroom without having to be cajoled or bullied into getting up seemed like a major breakthrough. Likewise, the first time she sat and read a book with Imogen and the first time she said she wanted to go down with Inge to fetch Annie home from school. We thought it best, when she first came out of hospital, to keep the girls mainly away from her, explaining that Mummy was still not well and they had to be very good and quiet around her. It was, naturally, difficult for them to set their mother to one side, as it were, and not relate to her in the way they normally did. As their mother came back to them, and they no longer had to tiptoe around her — in Imogen's case, literally, with a lot of comical hushing of her big sister as well — their return to their usual level of activity and affectionate involvement with the adults in the house started to lift the tense, funereal gloom that had rested over it. Annie mentioned that it was only two weeks to Christmas — without this seeming like a rather sick joke. There was a spell of fine, dry, if cold weather that helped. We took Bea out for a walk on a Sunday afternoon, which seemed to do her good. She actually seemed quite animated, walking with the girls, one on either hand, talking with them, and even laughing once as we were walking back to the car.

Professional life was, of course, on hold all this while. There had been flowers and cards from her publisher and agent when she arrived back from New York, and there were more when they learned she had been in hospital a second time. Phone calls came in regularly asking for progress reports. It marked another step on the way to recovery the first time I offered her the phone when Andrew, her publisher, called and she took it and spoke to him.

I knew she had nearly finished the final Meena book — or nearly finished the first draft — before she left for New York. I suppose everyone was worried whether she would be able to complete it and, in the longer term, where she would go from there. Did she have any new ideas? There were also financial questions about the longer term. I had done absolutely nothing about getting a job for weeks — not that there was any real sign that the employment situation was improving. I had also spent quite a lot of money on my dash to New York and in keeping things going while Bea was not in a fit state to write her usual share of the cheques. True, there was no immediate problem because I had had my salary in lieu of notice and my redundancy money, but if there were to be a split with Bea, if the final sign of her recovery was to take up from where she had left off in the plane and declare me *persona non grata* in her life, then things would look pretty grim.

There had to be a reckoning. This much I knew. While she was getting better, she treated me more or less as she treated Inge — as someone who was there and was instrumental in helping her, but had no especially close connection with her. I, in turn, treated her very warily. I assumed I must have played a causative role of some kind in bringing on her depression and prompting her to swallow the pills and vodka. I did not want to prevent her recovery or bring on some kind of relapse by forcing her to deal with me in any way that placed demands on her. But, as I say, she showed no inclination to accord me more than passing notice and when she spoke to me it was only ever about practical matters of the moment. I continued to sleep in the spare room. I wanted her to get better; I wanted her to be herself again. At the same time I was not sure what constituted 'herself' under the present circumstances and I dreaded the prospect that she might be regaining her strength merely in order to begin the final battle.

Christmas came and went — quietly. The New Year came and went, without any special celebration. We received a few invitations, including one from Mary and Jimmy in London, but Bea showed no particular desire for company yet, so I used the excuse of having no baby-sitter (Inge had gone home to visit her family in St Gilgen and do some skiing) to decline. My mother would doubtless willingly have come over, but I was trying to avoid parental complications on either side. Virginia had paid a visit on Christmas Day with the Major, but I took great care never to be alone with her and otherwise she studiously ignored me. At midnight on New Year's Eve, sitting alone with Bea at the opposite end of the sofa in front of the fire watching the usual jollifications on the television, I opened a bottle of champagne and proposed a toast 'Here's to next year — hopefully it'll be better than the last'. Bea clinked glasses with me once, drank a sip or two of the champagne and went to bed. I drank the rest of the bottle and tried to work out what I would say to her when the time arrived to work out where exactly we stood with regard to each other.

As I understood it, the position was as follows. Bea had declared effectively, if not in so many words, that she no longer loved me, hence our marriage, as far as she was concerned, could be no more than something to be lived with. It would be at best a matter of form, and at worst a millstone round her neck to be got rid of at the earliest opportunity. I did not believe that the thing with Antonio Perry was 'serious' to the extent that she was likely to leave me in order to be with him. If she had been seeing him for 'ages', I assumed this meant that their relationship went right back to the days when she was married to Rich

Guildersleeve ('be very nice to your husband's attorney' again), and that she had revived it and then kept it up on her visits to New York — or possibly when he visited London. Looking back, it was possible to imagine any number of opportunities she might have had to be with him.

But it seemed to me unlikely that she was counting on Perry to rescue her from me, in the way that she had perhaps used me to rescue her from her indeterminate state after the end of her first marriage, because, quite simply, I was gullible and Perry was not. She would not be able to manipulate him as, I was beginning to feel, she had manipulated me. It was more likely that he had been her bit on the side, her assurance to herself that her life with me was not her whole life, a way of keeping her options open, a reminder to herself that there was a world of men out there that she had thrived in before and might return to if ordinary domestic life proved to be less than fulfilling.

I assumed that she had reached the point of feeling less than fulfilled before she set out for New York but that, if she had not miscarried, she would probably not have provoked an open breach with me. We had had some of our happiest times, despite the obvious stresses and strains, through her two previous pregnancies and when the girls were very small babies. ... Or so I thought. What I now knew seemed to necessitate a total reassessment, of a very painful and humiliating kind, of the whole of our previous life together. Was any of the love she had shown me, any of the fulfilment she had seemed to get out of our relationship, the least bit genuine? I had no way of knowing, and I could not bring myself to cast everything we had had on the scrapheap. Better leave that question aside. When she lost the baby, she no longer had any incentive to keep me sweet in order to support her through the rest of the pregnancy ... or, more charitably, in the distress of losing the baby, she was no longer capable of keeping up a pretence towards me. Hence her rejecting behaviour in the hospital and on the flight home.

That more or less made sense. But why had she attempted to do away with herself?

Of course her depression must be largely physiological in origin, akin to postnatal depression. One or other of the doctors had said as much. Losing the baby was an appalling physical and emotional trauma for her. Perhaps it was unnecessary and impertinent to look for any other explanation. But, rightly or wrongly, the fact that it had been, thank God, a less than wholehearted suicide attempt apparently, prompted me to try and find some additional reason for it. If I could only understand Bea's motives, I might have a better chance of saving our marriage. That was what I wanted to do. I still loved her; I wanted to sort things out; I couldn't sort things out unless I understood her. With understanding, I might be able to make her see that we had a future together.

It might have been a cry for help. That is, after all, how deliberately unsuccessful suicide attempts are usually interpreted. She felt she was under intolerable pressure. She was being pressured to write a book she didn't really want to write — she had never put it in quite those terms to me, but it was quite possible that this was a factor. In addition, she was going through a bad patch in her marriage. In addition, she was entangled in a long-running affair that was essentially going nowhere. The last straw, she had a miscarriage. Everything was just too much — she flipped.

She might have done it to punish someone or to punish herself. She wanted to punish me for not giving her what she wanted, much as Inge's friend had ostensibly punished her boyfriend for deserting her. She wanted to punish Antonio Perry — this seemed rather far-fetched, for I had no idea whether Perry knew what had happened, though a pretty efficient grapevine seemed to operate on the other side of the Atlantic and floral tributes had arrived from America. Why?

Perhaps because Perry had mistreated her in some way, because Perry had made her lose the baby — what she had said on the plane possibly hinted at sex of a violent or acrobatic nature — or because he was not the sort of man who would do the white knight bit and ride to her rescue. She wanted to punish herself, because she had blamed herself for the miscarriage, possibly because she felt guilty about the affair with Perry, possibly — but, alas, it seemed only a remote possibility — because she felt guilty about what she had done or what she was going to do to me.

With cynical hindsight, I am inclined to suspect that if there was any guilt or blame going, Bea wanted it all, just as she seemed to want it all in other respects, the family, the children, the home and the exciting and varied sex life, the fame and the notoriety, the money come by relatively easily and the rags-to-riches myth. 'I behaved so shockingly, but I felt such enormous guilt afterwards, etc, etc.'

This did not enter my head at the time. When a relationship breaks down, it seems that one is condemned to constantly revise and rewrite the history of it. In any event, it seemed at the time that coming up with at least some fairly plausible explanations of what had been going on helped a little. On that basis, I felt that, when the time finally came, I would be better able to argue with Bea if she chose to argue, better able to persuade her if she needed persuading, better able to love and understand and forgive her if we were to make a go of it again.

But perhaps the psychiatrist she had been seeing had presented her with a completely different interpretation of her psychological state and its relation to recent events because, when we did eventually come to talk things over, her position was perfectly simple and straightforward: she wanted a divorce.

23

From the New Year Bea seemed to make more rapid progress. Inge returned — and I was very glad to have her back with us for the moral support she might give if things got difficult. Annie went back to school. Imogen started with a playgroup. Bea began to spend more time in her office, writing. She also answered all or most of the phone calls. She no longer needed to be persuaded to take her antidepressants, in fact I believe they were starting the process of reducing her intake. Things seemed to be going gradually back to normal.

Then one Friday in mid-January, after a flurry of phone calls during the morning, Bea came out of her office at lunchtime with a set look on her face as if she had made up her mind about something.

'Inge,' she said, as she came into the kitchen where Inge and I were making lunch, 'I want to talk to my husband. You can take the afternoon off.'

'Do you want me to pick up the girls, Bea?'

'No, I'll do it. I'm taking them straight down to my parents' house for the weekend.'

'But you haven't driven ...' I put in.

'I'm perfectly fit to drive. Thank you, Inge.'

Inge tidied up a few things and went out.

'Why don't you let me drive you down and pick you up again on Sunday?' I asked when Inge had gone.

'I said I'm fit.'

'It's a long way. You've been very ill. You're on drugs. I'll drive you.'

'I'll take *my* children to see *my* parents in *my* car, if I want to.'

'They're *our* children and I don't think it's safe. Don't worry, I'll just drop you there. I won't go in.'

'Nigel, you're not listening to me. I said I'm taking the children down to Wiltshire this afternoon, I don't want you anywhere near me or them. In fact, I don't want you to be here when we get back. I want you to get out of the house. I want a divorce.'

'What?'

'I think you heard me.'

'No! This is my house as much as yours. They're my children. I'm not walking out on them or it. Why are you saying this? Why are you doing this to me?'

'I want a divorce.'

'I heard you! … Why?'

'God, Nigel, isn't it obvious? I don't love you any more. You obviously don't love me. You haven't slept with me for months.'

'For God's sake, Bea, you had a miscarriage, you had a nervous breakdown!'

'You know that's got nothing to do with it.'

'It's got everything to do with it as far as I'm concerned. Christ, how can you say I don't love you?'

'Because I don't see any way, any way, you can possibly love me when you're screwing the au pair right under my nose.'

'What?'

'All those bloody walks, all those bloody picnics, all the bloody English tuition, the way she makes sheep's eyes at you all the time, you going off to the spare room, do you think I'm blind?'

'One of us is going mad here. I have not been screwing Inge. Ask her.'

'I have asked her.'

'You're lying.'

'I am not having you living in the same house with me and the girls and touching up some fucking Tyrolean trollop!'

'What has happened to you? Bea, calm down, listen to me. There is nothing going on between me and Inge. Why am I bloody saying this to you? I have got nothing to apologize for, there is nothing going on. May I remind you that on the plane back from New York you told me that you were having an affair with Antonio Perry, "fucking him up hill and down dale" I think was the expression. I have done nothing to you; you are bloody well breaking my heart!'

'You bastard!'

'I don't want any of this. Can't we sit down calmly and try and sort things ou?.'

'You lying bastard!'

'Calm down!'

'You fucking, lying, manipulating bastard, you fuck the fucking mountain woman, then you try and get out of it by accusing me. God, I should have seen this coming.'

'You are madder even than your bloody mother!'

'Are you going to beat me up like you beat her up? Don't you fucking try it!'

She grabbed a kitchen knife off the sideboard and waved it around in front of her. She seemed to have gone completely out of her mind. By contrast, I suddenly felt unreally calm.

'I'm not going to beat you up, but you're welcome to stab me if you like.'

'I want you out of this house.'

'I'm not going.'

'I'll call the police.'

'Fine.'

I turned my back on her and walked out of the kitchen.

'Bastard!'

She slammed down the knife and rushed upstairs. I sat down, still in a strange light-headed state of electric calm — unmoved internally, even peculiarly elated, and ready to react at any moment with lightning swiftness — while she ransacked the girls' rooms and stuffed a bag with things of her own, collected her laptop, dumped everything in her car, and returned for a parting shot.

'I want you out of this house by the time I get back.'

'I don't think you were listening, Bea. I said I am not going. I am not bloody going!'

'We'll see about that you … prickless bastard.'

And she went out slamming the door. My experience of Bea would have been incomplete if she had not animadverted at least once on the size of my penis.

* * *

I watched her drive off. She did not seem to be unfit to drive. She stopped at the end of our drive, waited for a car to pass, then pulled away at a normal speed. I had to assume the girls would be safe with her. To have raced round to try and get to them before she did would have served no purpose and only made more distress for them.

All my preparations for the moment of reckoning and sorting out had been in vain. It appeared that Bea only knew one way to end a relationship and that was to pick a flaming row with her lover, as with the South African by the lake, as with RT, as, for all I knew, with R. Guildersleeve esq., and perhaps in future with that pillar of the legal profession, Antonio Perry.

The telephone rang very shortly after she had left. It was her publisher.

'Is Bea there? It's Andrew Jacobs.'

'No, sorry, Andrew, she just left.'

'Really, she told me she would be there.'

'She's been very unpredictable lately.'

'Well, she's been under the weather rather, hasn't she? Can I leave a message?'

'I don't think you can, Andrew. She's left, as in she's leaving me, or rather, she's told me to get out. But as I've no intention of going, I think it's a fair guess she won't be back, don't you?'

'Are you all right?'

'No, Andrew, I'm not all right. My wife has just stormed off after threatening me with a kitchen knife and accusing me of sleeping with the au pair, whereas, in actual fact, she's been shagging her ex-husband's lawyer. So I think it's fair to say I've had better days. But then she has to get material to feed your insatiable appetite for Meena books from somewhere, doesn't she?'

'You're bloody drunk.'

'I wish I was.'

'Do you know where she's gone?'

'To her parents.'

'I'll phone her there.'

He rang off abruptly.

Gradually the light-headedness ebbed away and I began to assess the situation in a more sober light with the aid of a stiff drink. A premonition of the whole likely scale of the disaster rushed in upon me and I took another drink. By the time the police arrived, which was in the early evening, I was not at my sharpest and best.

'Mind if I come in, sir?'

'No, no. Sit down. Do you want a drink?'

'No thank you, sir.'

'What's it … what's it about?'

'We've had a phone call from a Major Williams — your father-in-law?'

'Lovely man — ex-army — surprised he remembered my name.'

'Yes, sir. According to him, you threatened your wife with a kitchen knife and threw her out of the house.'

'That's not exactly military precision, officer. She threatened me with a knife — but it was only a little one. Do you want to see it? Is it evidence?'

'That won't be necessary. Whose house is this, sir?'

'It's ours. It's partly mine. It's about one-third mine. The rest is my wife's.'

'I gather your wife's rather keen that you should not be here when she comes back on Sunday.'

'That's what she said to me too. Are you here to throw me out?'

'I'm sure you don't want any trouble, sir …'

'You mean I've got troubles enough already. "Nobody knows the trouble I'm in … Nobody knows, but … Jesus!" Louis Armstrong, officer, a very great singer.'

'Don't waste my time, sir. I'm not here to throw you out. I'm here to suggest you leave, as your wife said. Better that way than us having to come round with her when she comes back. Is there an Inge Scholtz here?'

'My wife gave her the rest of the day off. It was probably her last sane action.'

'Your wife wants her out too. It's none of my business, but shafting the au pair while the wife's in the house doesn't usually make for domestic harmony.'

'Did my wife say that too?'

'Your father-in-law, sir.'

'Can you give me one bloody good reason why you should believe what my father-in-law says rather than what I say?'

'Because he was bloody sober, sir, and you're bloody drunk. Don't try and go anywhere tonight. Get yourself sorted out and call in at the station tomorrow and leave a message with the desk sergeant that you're going.'

'What happens if I don't go? What happens if I stay in my third of the house?'

'We might have to arrest you on suspicion of threatening your wife.'

'She's stitched me up good and proper, hasn't she, officer.'

'None of my business, sir. Oh, and bring Miss Scholtz along too when you come to the station. Here's my card. You can get me on this number if you have any questions, but I hope I've made myself plain. Good evening!'

He left. I sat back down on the sofa and laughed at the pure bloody ridiculousness of it all.

***

I laughed on the other side of my face when I had to explain to Inge what had happened and that she had been summarily sacked for allegedly sleeping with me.

The poor girl was very upset. When I asked her if she had said to Bea that we were lovers, she vehemently denied it. 'She asked me if I liked you. I said I was fond — maybe I was very fond of you. That is all. Really, that is all. I think she must be crazy in the head. She makes up lies about us.'

Whether Bea had genuine suspicions or whether she just grabbed at an obvious pretext is neither here nor there. We talked it over until late in the night. Inge was very upset about leaving the girls, as she had grown very fond of them too. I was more than upset every time I thought about them, but I didn't know what to do. I had no idea what the legal position was. The only solicitor I knew at all was the London man who had done the conveyancing on the house for us. I managed to get hold of him at home by phone the following morning. He wasn't very happy at being called on a Saturday morning or very helpful. The gist of what he said was that it wasn't his area, but if Bea had asked us to leave and the police had asked us to leave as well, we had better go.

So we went. I had nowhere to go really, except to my mother's. I rang her to say I was coming, but she was out. I was in many ways more worried about Inge than myself, but she said she had friends she could stay with in London. We called at the police station and reported that we were going. I called at a cash machine and drew out a large amount of cash — fortunately, I still had a separate account. I gave Inge half of it, and gave her my mother's address and phone number and told her to write to me or phone me if she needed money or anything else — including if she had any trouble with the agency who had sent her to us in the first place. Then I dropped her at the station to take the train in to town. Waiting on the platform, I told her again how sorry I was that she had become mixed up in all this and been accused and lied about, and thanked her for the help she had given us. After all she had done for Bea during her illness, she had received the most appalling treatment. But she was very philosophical about it: 'I think maybe one year and a half is enough to learn English. I will go home soon and earn more money. I am sorry for you, Nigel. I think things will be really difficult.' When the train came in, I gave her a hug in farewell. She responded by kissing me on the lips. Whether that meant she was more than very fond of me, I don't know. Apart from sending her more money, and writing letters to the au pair agency on her behalf, I had no further contact with her and I have never seen her again.

I drove my car, which still had a large dent in the wing, though the headlights had been repaired, and which was laden with a couple of old suitcases, several black plastic binbags full of clothes, four cardboard boxes full of books and papers, and the family's third best computer, to my mother's house. I let myself in, made myself a cup of tea, and in the interval between my arrival and her return from an outing to a matinée in London with the Townswomen's Guild, I had time to reflect on the fact that, to all intents and purposes, I had no home, no wife, no children, no job, and no money and was back living in my parents' house. It seemed only a slight exaggeration to say that the whole of my adult life had been wiped out.

24

There are perhaps some respects in which it is more merciful to be completely wiped out or sent right back to square one then to be left languishing in some middle state. It can induce a kind of despairing elation and *je m'en foutisme* based on the fact of having nothing to lose. At least I knew precisely where I stood with Bea — and had enough mental strength to banish once and for all any thought of 'sorting things out', or pleading with her to take me back, or expecting her to come to her senses. I made a conscious effort also, in the early stages of my new-found deprivation, not to spend time attempting to work out why it had happened. That was something to reflect on in a time of greater tranquillity when the answers to the question might not hurt so much.

But the idea of total loss was no more than an idea. The children, in particular, were still mine. I had no clue as to how they were, how they had reacted to this latest upheaval, if they knew that I had been thrown out of the house, or what story they had been told to account for my absence when they returned home. I had not had the chance to say goodbye to them either, not that that mattered particularly because I was determined that I was not going to disappear out of their lives.

Determination, it soon became apparent, was a very necessary thing if I were not to lose contact with them.

On the Sunday, I rang 'home' at about the time I expected them to arrive back. There was no reply. I waited for an hour then rang again. Bea answered.

'Hello?'

'Can I speak to the children, please?'

'No.' She put the receiver down again.

I rang straight back. The phone rang the requisite number of times, then my own voice came on saying 'This is Bea and Nigel's number. I'm sorry … etc, etc.'

I put the phone down again and rang several more times with the same result. I then recollected that the answering machine broadcast the message it was receiving and recording aloud into the room. I rang again and after the introductory spiel and the tone said: 'Hello, Annie and Imogen, this is Daddy. If either of you is there, would you pick up the phone, and …'

This brought Bea back on the line.

'They're not here. Fuck off.'

'Where are they?'

'Fuck off!'

The next time I called her number I got the engaged tone. So, in for a penny in for a pound, I rang her parents' number.

'Hello?'

'May I speak to Annie and Imogen, please?'

'Who is that?'

'It's Nigel, Major. I'd like to speak to my children, please.'

'They're not here. You've got a bloody nerve. Where are you ringing from, a police cell?'

'Very funny, Major. Where are they, please?'

'Out of your hands, thank God. Don't ring here again.'

He put the phone down, so I rang him straight back. He picked up the receiver and put it straight down again. I gave him enough time, I hoped, to get comfortably settled in a chair, then rang again. This time it was the senior she-devil.

'Who is that?'

'Will you tell me where Annie and Imogen are, please, Virginia?'

'If you ring here one more time, I'll call the police.'

So I rang one more time — and their phone too had been left off the hook.

If these phone calls served one positive purpose, it was to convince my mother finally that the family I had married into comprised completely impossible people and to fill her with the same conviction as myself that we had a serious battle on our hands.

I assumed that the probability was that the children were back with Bea at Hill End. I assumed that the Major would have checked with the police that I had packed my bags and gone, and on that basis Bea would have felt it was safe to bring them back. On the Monday evening, I tried using the answering machine again to get a response. The phone went dead as soon as I began to speak and was then left off the hook. On the Tuesday evening, an official voice informed me that the number had been disconnected. When I tried directory enquiries for Anderson N., I was given the old, now useless, number and when I asked for Williams B., a new number, I was told that it was ex-directory. The Wiltshire Williamses were not answering their phone at all now. On the Wednesday morning, I rang Annie's school. The school secretary put me through to the headteacher, who informed me that Annie was not in school. Did she know where Annie was? No, she had not been told, and she had been specifically warned by Ms Williams that I might try and contact her and that she was to give no information about her whereabouts — not that she had any — in case I tried to abduct Annie. I also rang Bea's publisher and agent, who each gave me equally short shrift, and Mary and various other London friends, who were more sympathetic but unable to help. On the Thursday, I drove back to Ryehamstead, taking my mother with me as a witness in case I did anything that might be construed as a crime by hostile in-laws. I knocked at the door of the house, and there was no reply. I tried my key in the door, but the lock had been changed. I walked around to the back of the house; there was no sign of life. I knocked at the next-door neighbour's house. Their cleaning woman looked at me strangely and said she didn't know anything. When I came back, I found my mother in an argument with the retired couple across the way, whom, I must confess, I had made very little effort to get to know. She was defending me stoutly through the window of the car against charges of being a wife-beater and au-pair-molester.

'We've got Neighbourhood Watch here,' said Mr Soames, the old gentleman. 'He'd better not try anything.'

'It's my house, Mr Soames.'

'Well, we're keeping an eye on it while Mrs Williams is away. We'll call the police if he comes back,' he said, still addressing my mother as if I wasn't there.

'Disgusting! Disgusting! He ought to be locked up,' put in his good lady. 'And this is such a nice neighbourhood.'

My mother wound up the window. I got in the car. The old couple watched us until we rounded the bend in the road. My mother wept all the way back to Roxdon.

The next day I went to see a solicitor.

***

I contacted the solicitor as a precaution and to try and find out what my legal position was, but as I was not in a position to say that the children were 'missing' or 'had been abducted', both of which would have been police matters in any case, and as I had not been contacted by Bea or her legal representatives, there was not much that she could do, except to give me some pamphlets relating to divorce and the custody of children, explain the system of charges operated by her firm, and make me feel I was in the wrong profession by pointing out that she charged £100 an hour ... but, as I looked at my watch, that this initial consultation was free.

It was a week now since I had seen Annie and Imogen. I missed them very much. I hoped they missed me. I assumed they might be bewildered and upset. On the other hand, the recent months had been very eventful for them, so perhaps they had got used to upheavals to some degree. The Disgusteds of Ryehamstead had said that Bea was away. Presumably she had taken the children off somewhere, possibly to Wiltshire, possibly further afield. There was always the chance that they had been taken somewhere where there were paddocks full of ponies and other delights, and they didn't miss me at all. Was Bea in a fit state to look after them? Right up to the time of her abrupt exit, she had seemed to be still convalescing and had left the care of the children mainly to Inge and me. Had I made it clear enough to the solicitor that my wife might be mentally unbalanced?

I had time on my hands to worry over these and a thousand other questions, but there seemed very little that I could do. Until such time as Bea saw fit to make contact with me, or to make contact with someone who was willing to pass on information to me, it seemed that the only thing I could have done would have been to institute an official search for them — assuming that I could have persuaded the police that there was genuine cause for alarm. I did not think that would serve any useful purpose at this stage. I considered the possibility of driving down to Wiltshire and confronting the Williamses, if they were at home. If they were at home, and if they remained implacably hostile to me — which was a virtual certainty — then, even if the children were there, would I be able to force my way in to see them or would the children's presence compel their grandparents to behave in a reasonably civilized manner? I tried ringing them again. The phone rang and rang and there was again no reply. On the Sunday, I made up my mind and went to Hell Hall.

All the way there I stoked up my anger and indignation — who were these people to keep my children from me? Who did they bloody well think they were? But, as I entered the village, instead of carrying me to a climax, my wrath seemed to give way under me. It was froth, a bubble. My heart was beating wildly, but that was out of a mixture of hope of seeing the girls and apprehension at the prospect of a dreadful scene, not out of righteous fury. I hung around the place for a while hoping the children might show themselves and trying to ascertain whether there were any signs of life. Everything seemed very quiet. I walked along the lane at the back of the property to the gate into their back garden. It was bolted on the inside. Eventually I walked up to the front door and knocked. There was no reply. At the back, the dogs started barking furiously. I knocked again, again with no result. I went to look around the side of the house for a final check. As I did so, I heard a car coming up the drive.

It was not their car. The driver was a middle-aged woman who looked as if she must be a friend of Virginia's. She wound down her window. 'What do you want?' she said, without getting out of the car. 'This is private property.'

'I know,' I said. 'I'm looking for Major and Mrs Williams.'

'They're not here. I've just come to feed the dogs.' She looked at me suspiciously.

'Do you happen to know where they've gone?'

'Who are you? Why do you want to know?'

'I'm their son-in-law. I'm actually more interested in seeing my children, two little girls. Have they been here? Have you seen them?'

When I said who I was, she seemed to freeze momentarily. 'Nobody's here. You'd better go, now, or I'll report you to the police.'

'I'm only looking ...' I began, and made a slight move towards the car at which she hastily wound up the window, locked the door, and began hooting her horn for all she was worth, ' ... for my daughters.' She goggled at me through the car window, still furiously pressing the horn, with a look of mingled detestation and dread.

It appeared that I had acquired a reputation as a homicidal maniac across two counties. I gave up and walked away back up the drive at a dignified pace, struggling to resist the urge to turn around and attack her or her car, for she followed me as far as the entrance still blaring her horn.

The commotion had brought several people to their windows. A couple of men came running down the street. They spoke to the woman in the car who gestured in my direction. As I was getting into my car, which was parked a little way down the road, they left her and ran towards me. I hesitated with one foot inside the car and one on the road, about to lower myself into the driving seat. But by this time I *was* angry. I got back out of the car and waited from them.

They were both pretty hefty, probably father and son, red-faced, agricultural, and unfriendly. I think they'd expected me to jump in the car and drive off in a hurry. Shouting insults after a car is one thing, beating someone up in a village street — not quite in broad daylight, because it was starting to get dark — is another. Not that this would necessarily stop them, but at least it gave them pause.

'You get in that bloody car and go,' said the elder man. 'We don't want your sort round here.'

'What bloody right has your sort got to tell my sort what they can do and what they can't?'

'This is our village,' said the younger. 'You clear off.'

'What if I don't clear off? I'm not doing anything, I'm only trying to find out what's happened to my kids.'

'Well, go and do it somewhere else.' He moved forward until he was standing more or less nose to nose with me.

'We don't like men who attack women,' put in the elder.

'Well, call the police and get them to arrest me.'

'We might just fucking well do that,' said the younger, placing his boot over my left shoe and pressing down hard.

I pushed him in the chest to get him off, which was the cue for a brief scuffle, in which the elder one grabbed me from behind with his arm across my throat, the younger one punched me in the stomach a couple of times while I flailed at him with my arms and legs, and then they opened the car door and forced me inside. My right leg was left trailing over the door sill. The younger made as if to close the door on it. I got the point and pulled my leg inside. One of them then smashed something against the windscreen, which became completely opaque and starred with innumerable lines. They then stove it in from the outside, filling my lap and the passenger seat with gobbets of glass. Finally, grinning, they invited me to switch on the engine and bugger off out of their village. Which I did. The woman in the car, who had watched the whole business, sneered with triumph and gave me a V-sign as I drove past her and away.

I stopped in the nearest town to report the incident to the police. Their enquiries, if they ever made any, drew a blank. I called out a windscreen repair service — at vast expense, it being Sunday — and drove home, home to my mother's that is. Perhaps the most humiliating thing about the whole experience was that it was to my mother's I had to go to attend to my cuts and scratches and be fussed over in the process. It was the first of several occasions on which I wondered how much lower I could possibly sink.

25

But in the middle of the following week, however, there was hope. My mother went to answer the phone one afternoon and came rushing back saying 'It's the girls!'

'Are you all right?' – 'Yes, we're having a lovely time' – 'Where are you?' - 'In France' – Where in France?' – 'In Paris' – 'What are you doing in France?' – 'We've been to Disneyland!' – 'Oh lovely. Who with?' – Mummy and grandma.' – 'Oh lovely, when are you coming home?' – 'Soon' – How soon?' – 'We don't know. Mummy says we have to go now.' – 'Can I speak to mummy?' – 'Mummy says she's writing you a letter. Bye, Daddy. – 'Darling …' Then the phone went dead.

Mummy didn't actually write in person. A firm of solicitors wrote on her behalf, announcing that she was filing for divorce on the grounds of my adultery with Inge Scholtz and asking for the name of my solicitor.

This was no surprise — after all, Bea had said she wanted a divorce in the course of our final quarrel. Receiving official notification of her wishes was, nevertheless, something of a shock, as was the realization that she believed in her own version of events sufficiently not merely to spread rumours and blacken my name but to base legal proceedings on them. Surely her story would never stand up in court.

The first thing, however, was to secure some form of access to the children. I instructed my solicitor to write back and say that I would not enter into any discussion of divorce until suitable arrangements had been made for me to see the children and to be kept informed of their whereabouts. Like everything else in the dreadful and costly saga that then began to unfold, this took a lot of time and a good deal of wrangling to organize. Eventually, it was conceded that I should see them every other weekend. Even this was not without complications, for when I went to pick them up for the first time, not having actually seen them for over a month by then, I was not allowed inside the house. I had to conduct negotiations with the new au pair, a Finnish girl, who kept me cooling my heels for about twenty minutes until she appeared with Annie and Imogen. It was wonderful to see them again, and they seemed very pleased to see me, but they came just as they were, without any overnight things, and Annie said 'Mummy says can we be back by four o'clock'.

'Darling,' I said. 'We're going back to grandma's and you'll be spending the night with us there. I'll bring you back by four o'clock tomorrow.'

Annie looked rather doubtful about this. I asked the Finnish girl if she could get them some nightclothes, toilet things, etc. She then looked doubtful, so I asked to speak to Bea. No, I couldn't, Bea wasn't there. She didn't say this very convincingly. I thought about asking the girls if their mother was in the house, but this would have entailed putting them under pressure possibly to lie on their mother's behalf. I asked the Finnish girl again if she could get some night things. Bea, she said, hadn't said anything about that.

I knew my mother was longing to see the girls and had gone to some trouble to get things ready for them. I felt like taking them with me and damn the consequences. On the other hand, my recent attempts to be pro-active had not met with great success, and there seemed little point in further antagonizing Bea and possibly upsetting the children. The phrase 'see them every other weekend' was susceptible of various interpretations. In the end, I decided it was better to fall in with Bea's schedule on this occasion, but to inform explicitly beforehand that next time I would be collecting them on the Saturday and bringing them back on the Sunday.

So a good deal of that first reunion was spent in the car. And I also had to bear the brunt of my mother's disappointment and her repeated injunctions to stick up for myself and not let 'that woman' (as she now usually referred to Bea) have things all her own way. But that woman was showing a remarkable determination not to give an inch. When I went back two weeks later, after a verbal reminder to the Finnish au pair, and after writing a letter to Bea clearly stating my intentions, the girls were once again brought out with no overnight things and I had, more or less word for word, the same conversation with Tina (the au pair).

This time, however, after reminding Tina yet again what they were, I stuck to my plans. The results were, first, a vituperative phone call from Bea about an hour after the four o'clock Saturday deadline, unilaterally imposed by her, had passed, in which she simply screamed abuse and threats until I put the phone down on her, and, second, another visit from the police. Although the police were fairly easily reassured that the children were safe and that nothing untoward was going on — nothing, in fact, that their mother had not been explicitly informed about — and although they were perfectly polite and reasonable and left after a short time, it was nonetheless upsetting for everyone including the children that they should have become involved at all. If Bea could not actually stop me seeing the children, then she seemed to be resolved that I should not be left in peace to enjoy seeing them or they to enjoy seeing me. When I took them back to Hill End on the Sunday afternoon, arriving back at four o'clock precisely, the au pair hustled them inside immediately and the door closed behind them with a definitive slam.

A fortnight later again, when I turned up at what was becoming the regular time, there was no answer when I knocked on the door. I waited around for an hour or so — nobody came and nobody went and still nobody replied to my knocks on the door. I rang my mother to tell her that there was something up and that I would be late back, only to be informed by her that there had been a phone call from somebody called Tina, soon after I left, to say that they had changed their plans for the weekend and had all gone down to Wiltshire, but that it should be all right for the Saturday after next.

I simply did not have it in me to drive all the way down to Wiltshire again — enemy territory — to try and insist on my rights.

It was evident that Bea would take any and every opportunity to show who was boss, and that she would concede things only grudgingly and on her own terms. Since she had given instructions that nobody was to give me her new phone number, and she would not answer letters that I sent her, there was nothing for it but to go through the solicitors. After a good deal of negotiation, the original arrangement in regard to the girls was made more precise. I was to be allowed to see them every other Saturday for the day, but could only have them for the Saturday and the Sunday once every six weeks (apparently they had acquired various Sunday commitments that made more frequent Sunday visits impossible). But these arrangements did not necessarily apply during school holidays, and they would be reviewed if I stopped living with my mother, basically because I might not then have suitable accommodation to enable them to stay the night.

***

Bea subsequently wrote several magazine articles on divorce, including one memorably entitled 'How not to get screwed by your husband'. Unfortunately, this did not appear in time for me to benefit from its wisdom. Since, at least from where I was standing, Bea seemed to be far more experienced as screwer than screwee, I should have bought the magazine and read the article in order to see whether she got her material by describing what she did to me and working out the ways in which, with her superior intelligence, she would have avoided being shafted. I suppose it was more likely that she was drawing on a general pool of experience amongst victimized wives. In any case, at the time the thing appeared, I would not have wiped my arse on any paper that Bea had contributed to, so I never found out.

In fact, perhaps the most likely thing of all, I suppose, is that she wrote out of her own experience as a victim. It is not altogether uncommon for aggressors to pose as victims — except in Bea's case, I'm not at all sure that it was a pose. Because I had no contact with her, I had very little idea of how her mind was working. She was not behaving at all like the person I had known and loved over the past seven or eight years. I had my earlier experience of her to go on, and the new and wholly unpleasant experience I was getting now, but I could not say for sure whether she was deliberately and calculatedly contriving things that would hurt me, humiliate me, and make life generally difficult for me, or whether she sincerely believed her own version of events in which she was the injured party, betrayed and threatened with violence by the man to whom she had given the best years of her life.

I'm inclined to suspect the latter, but who knows. The divorce process is not designed nowadays to establish the fault of one or other party in bringing about the breakdown of a marriage. It is not intended either to reveal who did what to whom, or what the exact nature of the relationship was, or what happened to turn lovers into haters — except in the very broadest sense. It is simply a mechanism for sundering married couples at least one of whom no longer wants to continue with the partnership. All the 'interesting' questions — all the questions that you turn over and over in your mind as you try to work out what went wrong, what you did, what is making this person whom you loved and who seemed to love you treat you like shit — are irrelevant. Save all that for the analyst, or the counsellor, or a sympathetic friend, or work it out for yourself. You may be crying out for explanations, but the process doesn't have room for explanations or for crying out. Life seems to be full of narrow passages that you have to pass through, but can only negotiate if you leave most of your human baggage behind. Work life is often like that. It only takes part of you. The rest is not relevant to the task in hand.

It took me a long time to grasp this fact, so I ended up in a good many futile discussions with my solicitor — at £100 per hour.

Financially, I was in a bad way. I still had no job, I had run through most of the money that had come to me through being made redundant — and still had a large credit card debt to pay off resulting from my trip to New York. I was now drawing unemployment benefit and waiting for my savings, my 'capital', to dwindle away to the point where I should be able to apply for legal aid to cope with the solicitor's bills. Leaving aside the question of the girls, I had little choice but to stay living at my mother's … No, that is not really true. I could have moved out, but I lacked the will and the motive to do so. And I had nowhere in particular to go to. If I managed to get a job, then I should obviously go where the job took me. If the divorce came through, I would presumably get back the money I had put into the house and that should enable me to buy a place of my own somewhere.

As far as the divorce was concerned, it was not so much a question of 'if' as of 'when'. I did not actively want a divorce, much as I had not actively wanted to get married, but I was resigned to the fact that there would have to be one. After all that had happened over the last however many months, there was obviously no way we were going to get back together without a major change of heart on Bea's part, and the chances of that happening seemed negligible, and even if she had suddenly, and almost unimaginably, appeared in the guise of a penitent saying she had made a dreadful mistake and begging me to forgive her, would I ever have been able to trust her? Perhaps, even in spite of everything. I did love her. I did — and still sometimes do —

cherish the thought of the good, happy, and funny times we had together and imagine the family life we might have had as the girls grew up. But it didn't happen and I don't recall spending much time even fantasizing that it might.

Inexorably, then, the divorce process got under way. Bea, through her solicitors, had filed a petition alleging adultery. An adultery petition can only really succeed if the respondent and the co-respondent admit the fact. I certainly denied it. Whether they made any attempt to contact Inge, I don't know, but if they did she must have denied it as well, because they withdrew the petition. That seemed like a small success. They then petitioned again on the basis of 'unreasonable behaviour', the only other 'fact' establishing the irretrievable breakdown of a marriage on the basis of which an 'instant' or 'quickie' divorce — that is, one that goes through in less than two years from the date of the original separation — can be obtained.

Since one of the 'interesting questions' was 'what did I do?', it might appear that having 'unreasonable behaviour' alleged against one might bring some enlightenment. Unhappily — or perhaps happily — this is not generally the case. My automatic response was that I had not behaved unreasonably — at least I was not aware of having done so. It seemed that I had successfully defended myself against a false charge of adultery, why should I not now defend myself against this other charge, which appeared at least as unreasonable as any behaviour of mine?

My solicitor laid it on the line. No doubt she was acting in my best interests. Her name was Diana Peterson, she was in her early thirties, quite nice and sympathetic — at least, professionally so — but generally businesslike and tough-minded. She pointed out that the very best I could hope for would be to drag the whole process out over five years — during which time I would not get any money unless I could persuade a court that Bea should pay me maintenance. Did I want that? Want Bea to keep me? No, perish the thought.

Good, she said, because it almost certainly wouldn't happen. I could defend the petition ... Yes? But the courts generally started from the view that the very fact that one of the spouses had petitioned for divorce was a strong indication that the marriage had broken down, consequently the petitioner did not usually have to work very hard to prove unreasonable behaviour. In any case did I really want the details of my married life aired in court and could I afford the expense of mounting a defence? Even if I could get legal aid — which was unlikely — I would have to repay all or part of the legal costs out of any money I received from a settlement. Finally, not to defend the petition would not adversely affect the amount of the settlement or the question of custody of or access to the children. She rested her case.

The impression I received was that the guiding principle, from the court's point of view, was anything for a quiet life, and that respondents were powerless unless they could prove that they never went to the pub, never overspent, always put down the lavatory seat, and had denied their spouses nothing in the course of however many years. Patient Griselda, it seemed, would have had difficulty finding a leg to stand on. Accept reality, get it over with, take the money and try and start again.

Of course, this is not true. It is perfectly possible to say no, to dig in one's heels, to give oneself the satisfaction of making the other party fight all the way. I asked whether they had specified the nature of my 'unreasonable behaviour'. Apparently, they had not.

'Would you ask them to do me the courtesy,' I requested Diana, 'of telling me what I did?'

'Does that mean you do want to defend the petition?'

'How can I say until I know what I'm defending myself against?'

'There's no chance of sorting things out on an amicable basis?'

'How can it be amicable when I haven't spoken to my wife since we broke up except to be screamed at down the phone?'

'Yes, just try and take things calmly.'

'I can do passive, I haven't got much choice, but I can't do calm. This is ruining my whole life. I was perfectly happy until six months ago.'

'Yes. I can't do anything about that, I'm afraid.'

'Why? I don't know why. I don't know what went wrong. This all blew up out of nothing. Last summer we were an ordinary happy family. We were expecting another child, for God's sake. Everything was going well. Suddenly she turns against me.'

'I know, but ...'

'She told *me* she was sleeping with someone else. She threatened *me* with a kitchen knife!'

'So you say, but ...'

'Now she accuses me of unreasonable behaviour. Unreasonable, bloody hell!'

'Mr Anderson, please. You could file a cross-petition and sue her for divorce.'

'What would be the point of that?'

'Exactly. If you want me to, I'll ask them to be specific about the unreasonable behaviour. In the mean time, would you think carefully about whether you want to defend the petition or not.'

'But your advice is to give up and look cheerful.'

'I'm only your solicitor, I'm in your hands.'

'Whose bloody hands am I in then?'

'Mr Anderson ...'

* * *

Apparently, I had a tendency to become violent and threatening (the incident in the car, perhaps, the incident with Virginia, the incident with the kitchen knife), I had become 'excessively friendly' with the au pair in a way that soured relations generally within the family, I was completely unsupportive of my wife at the time of her miscarriage (possibly because I was more interested in the said au pair by this time than in her), moreover I was generally unappreciative and unsupportive of her work, which was the mainstay of the family since I was patently unable to support it myself in a sufficient manner, finally, I went out of my way to antagonize my wife's parents, to whom, as an only child, she was particularly closely attached. These and many other instances of general turpitude made it unreasonable to expect my wife to go on living with me. She had shown the depth of her alienation by attempting to take her own life.

'This is mostly lies and all garbage,' I said to Diana.

'Do you want to defend the petition then?'

'Is there any point?'

'I'm in your hands.'

'No, no, let her have her way. Just try and get me as much time with the children as you can and as much money for the house as you can screw out of her, and let's get the bloody thing over.'

This was doubtless the sensible thing to do, in the narrow sense. And in the broader sense? 'Good name in man and woman,' Iago tells Othello, 'is the immediate jewel of their souls.' What price does one put on one's good name nowadays? I felt I had been done a great injustice and felt bitter and resentful about it, but my conscience was fairly clear. My children were too young to understand the situation. My family supported me. Outside of that, nothing I had done or not done would resonate in the least in the wider community. I did not even feel that I had any friends to speak of at the time. The people in Bea's camp would not have been impressed. The world at large was completely uninterested in me — not, as it later turned out, in the events as refracted through Bea's creative vision, but in my own feelings. The permissive society does not judge very harshly — outside certain categories of heinous crime — nor does it judge very deeply. It loves scandal and titillation, and the titillation of outrage, and seems to value notoriety as much as fame. An adroit self-publicist (or someone with an opportunistic agent) might perhaps have laid claim to his fifteen minutes and his fifteen thousand on the back of Bea's subsequent revelations by stepping forward as 'Naughty Nigel'. Perish the thought! I kept my jewel in its case.

Not contesting the case did not mean that everything was plain sailing from then on. Bea was still disinclined to give anything away. I applied for her to buy me out of the matrimonial home for a sum equivalent to the equity of my old flat, adjusted upward to reflect the increase in house prices and my contributions to mortgage payments over the years. Bea's solicitors countered by claiming, among other things, that my pension entitlement was much greater than hers and that I should either commit myself to contributing to the girls' school fees or reduce the amount of the claim on the house to account for the fact that Bea would have to bear the costs of the girls' schooling alone. To say, as I did, that I was quite happy for the girls to be educated in the state system, cut no ice. (Caroline, the original Caroline who married RT and went into the law herself, later told me that a colleague, commenting on the previously fluctuating fortunes of the recorder before whom they both were appearing, remarked in tones of sympathetic horror that this now eminent QC had once been so close to utter penury that 'he had almost been forced to send his children to state school'. The legal profession evidently takes private education as the norm.) There was also a good deal of toing and froing over the question of my access to the children. As can be imagined, I was keen not only to get generous terms, but to get whatever terms were finally agreed sewn up tight.

The upshot of all these arguments was that, before the Decree Absolute was issued, Bea and I and our solicitors appeared at an informal hearing before a district judge to endeavour to resolve the outstanding issues. This was the first time I had actually set eyes on Bea since our separation, and the last time that I saw her while she was still nominally my wife.

I was quite shocked. She looked older and tired and, frankly, rather plain. I had expected her to blaze into the session with her blonde hair flying, dressed flamboyantly or provocatively to knock the judge off his feet and demonstrate to me precisely what I had been missing and was going to be missing for all eternity. Instead, she was dressed very simply, almost dowdily, and had her hair scraped back into a bun. She was also wearing glasses again instead of her contact lenses. She sat down quietly without saying a word and avoiding eye contact with me, despite my almost involuntary efforts to make eye contact with her. She said hardly a word throughout the proceedings, leaving her solicitor to do all the talking and answering questions put to her directly in the briefest possible form.

I won't say my heart went out to her, but I was struck by the possibility that I had been guilty of the kind of thing I accused her of — seeing only my own side of the question, being wrapped up in myself, not appreciating the trauma inflicted on the other person.

Diana, my solicitor, had urged me to remain calm and businesslike and to let her speak for me. She outlined our claims and put forward our arguments vigorously. If anything, I was half inclined to think these claims ought to be moderated somewhat, lest they seem too much of an imposition on the meek, ageing, worn-down woman sitting opposite me.

Bea's solicitor was an elderly, distinguished-looking man with a plummy voice, quite possibly another friend or contact of her father's. The judge addressed him as 'Sir Ronald'. The case he put for her went something along these lines.

Bea had been quite a high earner in her relatively brief career as an author, but it would be a mistake to think that she was in any sense a wealthy woman, or that her career prospects were assured. Authorship is a risky profession. Public taste is fickle; a writer can fall out of fashion as easily as he or she can become fashionable. And to these external risks are added internal ones. As a result of the combined distress caused by the events that had led to the break-up of the marriage, the miscarriage, the actual break-up itself, which had led to her suicide attempt (Sir Ronald's chronology was rather out), and prolonged divorce proceedings, his client was suffering from writer's block. He thought we probably knew what writer's block was …? (We did). She had not been able to write a word for several months, consequently, and could not say for certain that she would ever be able to write again. Hopefully, of course, she would recover and be able to use her splendid talent once again (for the benefit of humanity, he might have added — he didn't, but the implication hung in the air). But there was no absolute assurance that she would. Moreover, his client was no longer young. She was considerably older than her husband. Now, admittedly, he was presently unemployed. It was to be hoped that he was making some effort to find himself further employment and that he was not in hopes that a court would permit him to sponge off his wife for the rest of his life …

At that point Diana intervened to point out, with something of an edge, that I was not claiming maintenance, merely a fair share of the money accumulated in the marriage and invested in the house, that all professions were risky in this day and age — as witness my own unemployed state, furthermore that Bea was only just over two years older than me. It was not a marriage between a synthetically preserved matron and a toy boy.

But had her client shown any vigour in attempting to find new employment?

Yes, he had, but there were very few openings in publishing. And Sir Ronald's client was not the only one whose ability to carry on with a professional life had been affected by the distresses of marriage break-up.

But, he was incapable of finding a publisher willing to take him on, had he considered the possibility of finding employment elsewhere?

No, as yet he had not. But he doubtless would if he had to and if, God forbid, Sir Ronald should ever find that his supply of clients dried up, would he consider stacking shelves in Tesco's as an alternative?

Diana seemed to be getting more heated than was perhaps professionally appropriate. The judge seemed to think so. He stirred in his seat. It occurred to me that I had made an elementary error in assuming the judge would be a man (though, in fact, he was) and that Bea had wisely chosen not to come in looking flamboyant or provocative as that would have cut no ice with a woman presider. But, then again, the solicitors presumably knew who was going to preside anyway.

His own alternative methods of supporting himself were irrelevant, Sir Ronald continued smoothly, he simply hoped that, though her client had not shown himself to be a particularly good provider for a family in the past, he would at least be able to provide for himself in the future, and, if he might be allowed to continue, he would finally point out that not only his client but also the two children, for whom she would become mainly, if not wholly, responsible, should I remain unemployed, had become accustomed to a comfortable lifestyle and that it would be in no-one's interest if it became difficult for them to maintain it. Bringing up children was a long and expensive business to which the former husband had a duty to contribute as far as he was able, and to provide against the possibility that he might not be able to contribute for some time to come, the sum that his client should pay to become sole owner of the matrimonial home should not be unduly large.

The judge seemed to feel the force of Sir Ronald's presentation. At least, he weighed in discreetly on their side over money, but counterbalanced that by suggesting that our proposals regarding the children were perfectly reasonable. After some haggling, it was determined that my share of the house, valued at £350,000 at that time of still fairly low prices, was £50,000 and that I should pay £150 a month for the children's maintenance while I was unemployed and £300 a month when I returned to employment, the latter figure being adjustable, depending on my income and the circumstances etc, etc. The existing arrangements for access to the children were confirmed, with the addition that I should be able to take them on holiday for a week every year and have them for Christmas one year in three.

The judge left; Sir Ronald left with Bea, who looked me once in the eye on parting, though what the significance of the look was I could not determine; Diana repacked her briefcase slowly.

'I'm sorry,' she said, with unlawyerly candour, 'I did my best, but we probably should have done better. That bastard Sir Ronald really gets up my nose.'

'Oh well,' I said, glad now to have the thing over and thinking that £50,000 was quite a lot of money and that at least I should still get to see the children once a week. 'It could have been worse.'

'What did you think of your wife?'

'I was quite shocked actually. She looks as if she's been having a hard time.'

'No make-up, hair tied back, dressed down, glasses — does she usually wear glasses? — doing her best to look her age and more, wouldn't say boo to a goose. Straight out of dear Ronald's handbook for distressed lady petitioners. Don't waste any sympathy on her. I hate women who play the victim. Come on, I've just got time to buy you lunch before I'm due back in Hertford.'

She was right, of course, about the strategy, Bea's or Sir Ronald's. And the writer's block did not last very long either. A month or two after the decree was made absolute, 'Death, Divorce, and the Whole Damn Thing: Bea Williams tells her story' appeared in a glossy magazine, and shortly after that Meena Mark 4 finally made it into the bookshops, the heroine meeting a grisly end on the orders of the Mob in winter in Chicago, and appearing on the last page with her throat cut, her blue eyes still open and her hair and her legs spread wide, visible beneath the ice near the shore of one of the Great Lakes.

Afterwards

From the perspective of eight years on, it ought to be possible to take a more balanced view of events. But 'the waste remains', as William Empson writes — there is still bitterness, and to this day I do not fully understand why everything fell apart so suddenly. But, without getting inside Bea's head, I don't see how I could ever grasp it entirely. The waste remains, but it does not usually actually kill. Rather than dwell analytically on the past, I ought at this stage to count my blessings, enumerate my achievements, and generally endeavour to raise my self-esteem a couple of notches.

I have good relations with Annie and Imogen. The former, now fourteen, takes after her mother more in looks, is generally more temperamental and adventurous, and could be a handful through her teenage years. The latter, eleven, quite a shy and quiet girl, but very sweet-natured, takes after me more in looks and gets on particularly well with my mother. Both girls seem well-balanced (within the normal parameters!), and neither seems to have suffered unduly from being brought up by a celebrity mother who goes away quite frequently. Who knows, they may even have gained from having a succession of young women from all over the globe helping to look after them. Neither of them seems likely to replicate with Bea the tortured relationship that Bea had with her mother — one person I shall continue to go out of my way to avoid at any function that brings all the generations of the family together. All this is good, yet I cannot but miss day-to-day involvement with them. So much happens between meetings of which I have no intimate sense or knowledge. It is as though children whom you do not live with are suddenly propelled into the same status as adult children who have left home. I recollect how eager my mother was for any crumb of news from me when I was at university and how sparingly I provided those crumbs. Annie and Imogen are more forthcoming — I'm probably lucky that they are girls — but the situation is rather the same.

I have a new partner and another child. I have made some new friends and have recently rediscovered some old ones. I have a job; I am not a pauper; I partly own a house; I can hold my head up modestly in bourgeois society ... It begins to sound like one of those all-purpose Christmas letters.

Getting a job, after being out of proper work for the best part of two years and — it might have gladdened Sir Ronald's heart — driving a van for a local company for several months just so as to get out of the house and not be totally idle, enabled me to start rebuilding my life. I took a job with a publishing company in Oxford — not the one that interviewed me while I was still with Bea — in a position and at a salary not too far below where I was when I was downsized the first time. I am still in reference books. I doubt whether I shall ever get out of that niche or rise to a senior managerial position, but who knows and so what.

I moved out of my mother's house soon after getting the job and bought a small anonymous house in Oxford off the Cowley Road. My mother was loath to see me go and, since she had been an unfailing source of support through the difficult time, I felt somewhat guilty at going. She began to talk about moving to Oxford soon after I got there. I discouraged her. It was not simply that I was still powerfully aware of the precariousness of all professional and domestic life, I had to admit (to myself, not directly to her) that I did not want her there. I had visions of myself following her into old age still apparently tied to her apron strings.

That situation was, fortunately, resolved when Dave, Maisie, and their by then three children decided to move south again. My brother was still actively Green, and Red, but the organization he was working for was keen for him to move to its headquarters in London. With the most egalitarian principles in the world, the problems of swapping a tumbledown cottage in Lincolnshire for reasonably decent accommodation in the London area for a family of five were enormous — and Maisie was beginning to talk about 'having put up with' the green and simple life for more than ten years, whereas in earlier days she had been as wholehearted an advocate of it as Dave. My mother considered the possibility of asking them to move in with her, but the prospect of sharing her living space with two appalling housekeepers and three active and not very domesticated children — dearly as she loved them — did not greatly appeal. After much debate within the family, it was eventually decided that she would make over her house to them and buy a ground-floor flat nearby with a small garden. This was quite complicated to organize financially, but in human terms the arrangement seems to work reasonably well. My mother has her independence, but is near to her richest source of grandchildren, and I too am near enough to drive over and assuage her feelings if they need assuaging because some change has been made to her old home that 'with the best will in the world' she cannot approve.

* * *

As it seemed that I should never have any professional input into fiction, and was no longer able to help Bea with her plots, I at last found an outlet for my wish to be somehow creatively involved with literature by writing children's stories. These grew, in classic fashion, out of stories I made up for Annie and Imogen when they were little. Imogen, miraculously, remembered there had been a story about a white lion, even though she had fallen asleep in the middle of its first telling. She often asked for it. I began to expand my repertoire and eventually to write them down. I did not think at first of trying to get them published.

The best of them are now in print, but the more important aspect of my children's writing as far as I am concerned is that it forms a bridge between my old family life and my new one. Some of the stories grew out of being with Annie and Imogen, some out of missing them, and altogether they were instrumental in bringing me together with my present partner, Sophie. She was a divorced art teacher in her thirties who had trained as an illustrator but had nothing much to illustrate; I was a divorced publisher's editor in my forties dabbling as a children's writer but totally unable to draw or paint. We were introduced by mutual friends — spare man meets spare woman again and shades of the unfortunate Jill — but we hit it off well, cautiously developed a friendship, gingerly advanced into sex, warily circled around coupledom, procrastinated over moving in together, keeping separate establishments for a long time, and debated endlessly over whether we should have a child, though we both wanted children. To date, we have Tom and are very happy though, in saying so, I feel that we both keep our fingers firmly crossed behind our backs.

* * *

Our modest success as a book-producing partnership is dwarfed by Bea's continuing popularity both as an author and as a general media celebrity. I assume she wanted fame — fame spiced with a modicum of notoriety. She used to be greeted by Michael Parkinson and his studio audience as a welcome returnee; she has been on *Desert Island Discs* – Bob Dylan, Cole Porter, Elton John's *Candle in the wind*, Edith Piaf, *I'll be glad when you're dead, you rascal, you* ('for my mother'), Abba, *The minute waltz* ('if there's a version with wrong notes it'll remind me of my girls'), *The ride of the Valkyries*, 'not the Bible, thank you, I'll take the *Kama Sutra* instead,' and Tennyson's poems; she is frequently pictured in *Hello* and other magazines of the sort that you find in dentists' waiting rooms, either in a group of rich women with double-barrelled names or with a tanned *glitterato* hanging on her arm. She is rumoured to be contemplating an alliance with either a Welsh life peer or an Italian film director. If she does marry the life peer, I confidently expect her name to appear in an honours list before long. Assiduous readers of such magazines or watchers of chat shows may have been able to pinpoint the precise moment at which she had her face lifted.

She hasn't yet won the Booker Prize, but it might come. She has real talent, I think. She finally wrote her book about Hell Hall (called *Hell Hall*), and it was good; much better than her sensationalized account of our divorce, *Out of the Depths*. She was nominated for *Hell Hall*, but didn't get the prize. The way these things seem to go, she might well have won it the following year as a compensation, but, thankfully, the nominating committee had the same low opinion of *Out of the Depths* as I did. (But then, I wouldn't appreciate a portrait of myself as a kind of latter-day, Viagra-swallowing, knife-wielding Soames Forsyte from Pontypridd, who buggers the au pair while one of the children is being run over by a lorry, would I?)

Neither of these novels brought in quite the mountainous revenues, however, that her agent and publisher wanted. And at their behest — and that of her adoring fans — she was forced to resurrect Meena … when the ice melted in spring, Meena's body double was fished out of the lake in a blonde wig.

One feature of the media and information age is the longevity of dross. Even if she never fulfils her promise as a serious writer, one could safely predict a lengthy half-life for herself, her books, her life-story, and her one-liners amid the mass of trivia.

This judgement may seem a little ungracious, for, once the divorce was over, her hostility towards me seemed to abate. She has never put any serious obstacles in my way as regards seeing the girls; she has been generous in the financial way, never making even the full demands on me that she would have been entitled to make under the settlement. After a year or so had elapsed from the divorce, she began to be quite nice to me on the rare occasions that I encountered her when collecting or bringing back the children. For her even to ask 'How are you?' seemed to be a great step towards amicability after the way she had kept herself hidden and only communicated via the au pair in the early days of our separation. But I cannot find it in my heart to warm towards her again. There is a kind of shutter that comes down when I see her, even though she made one significant attempt to melt the ice between us.

I happened to go to a bookshop in London on a day when she was there signing copies of *Reichenbacher's Fall*, the account of the resurrected Meena. When I saw the banners in the window, my first instinct was to go elsewhere. I had not seen her for about two years before that, partly because she still spends quite a lot of time in America, and partly because the publication of *Out of the Depths* had increased the coolness I felt towards her to glacial coldness and made me actively avoid coming into contact with her. Nevertheless, after some hesitation, a kind of bitter curiosity got the better of me, and I went into the shop.

It was before her face-lift and she was looking a bit pouchy. She had also put on some weight. Her hair was still long and blonde — probably with help from the bottle. She has latterly been modelling herself on Mae West and Bette Midler, as this fits the image most readers have of the author of the Meena books and goes down well on chat shows. She was wearing a sort of stole over her shoulders and a low-cut dress showing off her now ampler charms, and joshing with the punters as they presented their hardbacks to be signed. I should have taken a look and gone, but instead it came into my head to be a momentary spectre at the popularity fest. I picked up a paperback copy of *Out of the Depths* and joined the line.

When the tall man in front of me presented his copy of *Reichenbacher's*, Bea asked in a sort of mid-Atlantic drawl 'Is it for you, big boy?'

'No,' he said, 'it's for my wife. Would you mind putting "To Celia, Here's looking at you, kid". And would you sign it "Meena", please?'

'That's a man's line, honey. That's Bogart's line.'

'Is it? I thought it was from one of your books.'

'Shall I put "To Celia, send your husband to the cinema"?'

'No, just … if you wouldn't mind.'

'You're the boss!' She scrawled the message on the title page, and handed him the book. He checked it, presumably to reassure himself she hadn't written anything uncomplimentary, and turned away forgetting to say thank you.

'Jesus!' said Bea under her breath to the bookshop representative who was standing beside her and handed him a glass to refresh. It was my turn.

'What shall I …?' she asked, as I put my copy down in front of her. Then she recognized me.

'You're the boss.'

For a second she seemed fazed, even slightly embarrassed. Then she wrote something quickly, closed the book, handed it to me with the briefest of eye contact, and turned her attention to the woman behind me, who was on tiptoe and about to gush.

'Ms Williams, I think your books are so wonderful. It is such a privilege …'

I looked inside the cover and read 'I get out of here at 3 … ?'

I waited.

Shortly after three, she finished signing, was profusely thanked by the staff, refused their offer to call a taxi, and walked to the door amid a small ripple of applause from fans who were still in the store, signing a couple of autographs on the way. I joined her on the pavement outside.

'Thank God, that's over' she said in her normal voice. 'It's nice to see you. Drink, coffee?'

'Not really.'

'Well, I need something. Please?'

I shrugged my shoulders and followed her into a café.

'I did it mainly for the money,' she said after we had sat down, 'nothing personal. I know it's crap. It's a treadmill, you know. I've been on it so long I ought to be fit as a bloody flea. I'm not. Did you read it?'

'Yes.'

'I was going to send a message via the girls not to. Sorry. Was there anything about the girls? You have been seeing them, haven't you? I've been away again.'

'They're fine. I read it because I thought it might help me understand ...'

'It's cheap fiction, Nigel, that's what I do.'

'Not entirely. I thought the thing about your parents was good.'

'Did you? Well, you would, wouldn't you? Did you really?'

'Yes.'

'Thank you. I value that, coming from you.'

'Don't mention it. Bea, I have never understood why ...'

'Just hate me, if it makes it easier for you. I don't particularly want you to hate me, but I could say you have a right to. I'm thinking of writing a book about Estella — you know from *Great Expectations* — anything to get away from fucking Meena. She was brought up to be Miss Havisham's revenge on men, you know, Estella was. I expect that's what my mother did to me, subliminally, of course. Dumping men is what I seem to do, and it makes very good copy. The women lap it up, so do a lot of men. It's why I'm so frightfully popular. So I extend the right to hate me to all the men I've actually dumped. I always have. You don't still love me, do you?'

'No, I don't. I can say that with certainty. I don't.'

'Fine, good. How's your new woman? The girls say she's nice.'

'She is.'

'Well then, I'm glad for you. And we still have the girls. We could, as they say, still be friends.'

'I don't think so. We can be polite.'

'That's a strange thing to say. To come all the way to London and drag me out of a signing session to say "we can be polite". You could be nice to me, Nigel, that's what you do — and you do that very well, and I'm not being sarcastic, and I'm not ungrateful for … for the past. I will say I'm sorry — once. OK? Sorry. Now it's up to you, hate me or be nice.'

'I'll think about it.'

'Don't think about it too much. That's probably your besetting sin. Now, if you'd be nice enough to get me a taxi, I'll trouble you no more. Is it this weekend you're seeing the girls or next?'

'Next.'

I called her a taxi.

It was not in her power, alas, to trouble me no more. In order to get over a fit of renewed bitterness following this meeting, I began this account.

* * *

I recollect once hearing a man at a dinner party complaining at length about a trip he had recently been on to somewhere in North Africa — a filthy place, according to him, and full of filthy people. The main actors in his story were fleas. He had gone to a hotel in X and found it was full of fleas, then to a hotel in Y and it was full of fleas too, finally, and in desperation, he had moved to a five-star hotel in Z and —

what do you know? — there were just as many fleas there, and because it was a five-star hotel they bit even more fiercely. To which I made the retort — which seemed witty at the time — that if everywhere I went I found there were fleas, I should draw the obvious conclusion about myself.

It has sometimes, ruefully, occurred to me that I have gone the wrong way about things in trying to fathom the workings of Bea's mind and character. Perhaps I ought rather to examine the pattern of my own life and to consider the possibility that if RT had got bored with me as a friend, and if Hilary had got fed up with me as a lover, then it must follow as the night the day that, over the long term, Bea would tire of me as a husband. I must simply be a boring and inadequate person.

I can only hope this is not the case and that the recurring pattern in my life is not one of attaching myself to people who in the end reject me. I do not know if there is a thread forming a pattern in the individual life — and if there is, one could only know it, and know it to be complete, I suppose, on one's deathbed. Long — and usually reluctant — as my professional contact with the writings of business people has been, I have never learned to be properly businesslike in my dealings with the rest of the world, but that is not to say that I have learned nothing. Since, according to my brother, my nature is to quote, quote, and quote again, I can shamelessly offer this insight, which I like, from a distinguished industrial gentleman called Sir Dominic Cadbury who said: 'There is no such thing as a career path; it is crazy paving, and you have to lay it yourself.' Sound wisdom for the modern world of business, and how very like life in general, you may say — though it doesn't all fit together very easily, no-one is entirely the paver of his or her own path, and it often feels as if you are haphazardly covering over a small bald patch in time rather than building something that leads somewhere or forms a feature in the great universal garden.

One other thought occurs to me. Just as, for some people at least, there used to be a linear career path, so for most people of previous generations there was a linear life path. In one relatively short lifespan, the average person would normally expect to have one experience of all the major life events, one go at all the big challenges, one season of youth and beauty, one life partner, one set of children, one occupation, etc. etc. Thanks to increased longevity, changing social circumstances and easy divorce, cosmetic surgery, flexible employment, choice in everything, and sundry other blessings, this is no longer the case. You get several bites at the cherry. If at first you don't succeed you can try again. It is almost though reincarnation were possible on earth in one lifetime, and perhaps merit gained or lost in one span of domestic or professional existence may even entitle you to a better or worse deal in the next.

In these circumstances, the questions that have occasionally preoccupied me while trying to make sense of things may need rephrasing. A recurring pattern there may be, but a lifelong thread? There is little possibility of a whole life fitting together and growing organically to a meaningful point. There are fewer opportunities for a life's work or a lifetime's achievement, but more for a lifetime's learning, and more chance of applying some of the wisdom acquired by experience when similar circumstances recur. More room for improvement, more space to fail and retry without quite the same awful sense of time's winged chariot bearing down on you. This has to be a good thing, doesn't it?

Certainly, many recent changes are for the better. Improved communications, for one thing, make it easier to keep in touch with Annie and Imogen who both have mobile phones and can use e-mail. They also enabled me to get back in touch with RT, whose whereabouts I finally rediscovered via a search engine on the Internet. It turned up an Arthur Llewellyn James in the biology department at the University of Wales. I wrote a letter to this virtual person saying that, if he was the RT James with whom I had shared a room at university etc ... would he like to get in touch? He did and we have become friendly again and see quite a lot of each other.

As I mentioned before, we have talked about Bea — usually while doing a bit of bloke bonding in the pub, leaving Caroline and Sophie at home with the children. He was, as I said once before, amazed to discover that I had actually been married to Bea. He had all her books and watched her television appearances — when he could do so without Caroline knowing about it.

'I don't think, I could ever have lived with her,' he said, 'I've got to hand it to you, Nige, you've got one over on me there. And she really humiliated me, you know. I felt smaller than my own prick. But, on the other hand, she did give before she took away. I mean, for God's sake don't ever say this to anyone, especially not ...' and he leaned over confidentially, as if Caroline might walk into the pub unexpectedly, 'she was definitely, but indubitably, the best fuck I ever had. You don't mind me saying this, do you? It was all premature ejaculation ... before you were married, that is. And, God, she was a lively thing in those days — you know, so colourful, so sharp. I don't regret it. I expect she's forgotten me — though I actually thought the chap in *Out of the Depths* was more like me, perhaps, than like you. Pontypridd, you know, a bit of a fighter. Anyway, I don't regret it. Mind you, I realize she put you through the old sausage machine a lot more than she ever did me. But if I hadn't known her, if I hadn't had her, I'd have been the poorer for it — you know what I mean?'

And perhaps, in the end, I could, with many, many reservations and a good deal of grudging, just about agree with that.

www.ingramcontent.com/pod-product-compliance
Lightning Source LLC
Chambersburg PA
CBHW061145170626
46809CB00003B/993